Jobeth

BY
MONA FITCH-ELLIOTT

Copyright © 2024 by Mona Fitch-Elliott

All rights reserved. This book or any portion thereof may not be reproduced or used in any manner whatsoever without the express written permission of the publisher except for the use of brief quotations in a book review.

Printed in the United States of America

First Edition, 2024

HARDBACK ISBN: 979-8-8691-7349-2

PAPERBACK ISBN: 979-8-8691-7347-8

EBOOK ISBN: 979-8-8691-7348-5

Red Pen Edits and Consulting, LLC

www.redpeneditsllc.com

TABLE OF CONTENTS

From The Author		1
Dedication		2
Introduction		4
Foreword		5
Part One	Filled To Overflowing	8
Part Two	Blessed Are The Poor	28
Part Three	Mount Up On Wings Like Eagles	62
Part Four	Cry Out Like A Woman	80
Part Five	Holy Song In A Strange Land	106
Part Six	Finding Shalom	142
About The Author		179

FROM THE AUTHOR

In the Bible, the "Book of Job" chronicles the trials and travails that befall a man who loves Yahweh. Through all manner of profound loss, spiritual torment, and complete social alienation, Job keeps his faith. All of the many blessings of Job are stripped away. The man Job is left with only his relationship with God. *Jobeth*, the title of this work is a linguistic reflection of the King James Version of the Old Testament, with the suffix *-eth* turning the namesake *Job*, into Job*eth*. God giv*eth* and God tak*eth* away, not only from the man, but also giveth Jobeth, a woman, and taketh away from her as well.

DEDICATION

This story is dedicated to my writing group, my sisters, my daughters, and my mentors and supporters, who inspired me over the years.

"*Jobeth's* courageous and besieged protagonist, Tanya, takes the reader on a transformative journey through her precarious life as a jobless Pastor on the edge of homelessness in a poor New Jersey neighborhood to the war-torn land of Cameroon and back. In *Jobeth*, the author has created the vivid, authentic world of a strong andnpowerful woman exploring the meaning of faith amid the trials and tribulations of her life. I grew to care about and root for Tanya from her lowest moments to her triumphs—as she rekindles her faith and finds a special kind of love in a most unexpected place."

Elena Schwolsky

Author of Waking in Havana: A Memoir of AIDS and Healing in Cuba

(She Writes Press, 2019)

"An epic retelling of one of the greatest stories of all time".

Felicia Morrisey

Teacher

INTRODUCTION

Of course, women have been stripped and reinvented; they have been recreated spiritually and physically, throughout history. They have their particular stories in every age and culture. In our age, an African American woman finds she is left with only her relationship with God. In her estimation, she had been fortunate to have everything: a perfectly *blessed* life. She had her faith and family, and moreover, she was blessed with material: home, cars, and a degree of financial comfort. It comes to pass that she is reduced to her lowest foundations. Through it all she is determined to keep her faith and to keep believing and listening for her spiritual direction. She claims the blessing as it is bestowed.

The biblical Job insisted he was good and there is no reason for anyone to believe otherwise. In a departure from that perspective, Tanya, the central character of Jobeth, is no angel and never pretends to be. Even if there is an expectation of some kind of ordained saintliness, it turns out that she is only who she is and who she becomes.

"I will praise you, for I am fearfully and wonderfully made; marvelous are your works, that I know very well."

Psalm 139:14

FOREWORD

Mona Fitch Elliott and I knew each other before we met at seminary. We found out that our mothers worked together with the mother of author, Gloria Naylor. All four of us read Gloria's *The Women of Brewster Place*. Didn't you? Gloria Naylor is gone too soon.

I am not surprised that Mona wrote this book about all the ways *Tanya, a* Black woman, is challenged in the the US, Paris, and in Africa. We visited South Africa and Namibia together with our seminary and witnessed their suffering and resiliency. They believed that God could end apartheid (racism) with a snap of God's fingers. Their faith had left an indelible mark on us. Mona delivered a sermon while we were in the Motherland. We both danced with the people in church, school, community, and neighborhood gatherings while visiting.

This story, *Jobeth,* makes you ask "what?" "What's going to happen next?" So much happens that we cannot even imagine. The good, the bad, the ugly. Can she recover from this next conundrum? I just had to keep on reading to see where her life unfolded at the end of the book. Very satisfying.

Yes, I stayed up late to find out just what happened to this very real and remarkable Black woman. You may find part of your story in this book. Maybe you will see a sister, mother, or auntie. Maybe you will see she, who is dormant in your life. I think you'll want to take this great ride with Jobeth that Mona Fitch Elliott maps out for us with tender care and humor.

Be encouraged!

Ramona Cecille Navarro Daily, ELCA deacon, retired hospital chaplain and educator

February, 2022

MONA FITCH-ELLIOTT | 7

PART ONE

Filled To Overflowing

Her eyes were closed tight for this last landing and Tanya could feel the pressure of falling fast. Her ears were wrecked, as the plane made its descent. When she felt the wheels touch down on the runway, she opened her eyes to see that it was bright and sunny through the sandy dust that flew up around the plane. A smile played across her face, and she was overcome with a mixture of fear, joy, and excitement, like a schoolgirl, even if she was pushing 50 years of age. At this late date, she was actually in Cameroon. As she gathered her belongings, she wasn't sure if it wasn't all a dream. It took a few minutes to get her head and body together after being in the air, and this was a strange feeling indeed with so many unfamiliar sights and sounds, as she came into the Yaoundé airport terminal. The signage everywhere she looked was in French. She understood and that in itself was something. She could finally say that after a year of struggle, she knew another language besides English. The time she had spent living in Paris and attending classes, studying day and night, had prepared her for this moment, so she would understand.

Tanya was 48 but most people guessed she was in her mid-thirties. Several of her friends said she looked even younger since she left her job at New Creation Church in Chatsworth, New Jersey. Her dreadlocks had grown past her shoulders and her smooth skin was the color of coffee with cream. The struggle with her weight was constant mostly because she remembered a time when she was skinny, and she was always trying to get back to that place. She was not fat, but self-perception rules. Tanya's smile, her warmth, her compassion, and her competence defined her in ways that she was not fully aware. She had a great voice that served her well as a speaker and communicator, even if it was laced with the flavor of North Jersey and New York. While she was self-conscious about her appearance, she had tremendous presence and people were generally drawn to her.

She must have been easy to recognize from her pictures which had been sent ahead. A party of colorfully dressed men, women, and children, were waving wildly at her as some of them held onto a huge sign that had her name printed on it in bold letters. She was reminded that there were other tribal languages about which she had no clue. At least now she knew that she could still learn new things and she would go on learning it seemed. Africa at last...so far away from home... a whole new world and yet, of course, it is the ancestral home to Africans in Diasporas around the world.

She remembered when she had first come to Africa in 1985 with a church group more than five years before. They had come on a study tour and had visited 20 cities in the space of about 4 weeks throughout South Africa and Namibia. It was unforgettable. This time it would be different. Now she was *home,* not only because of heritage but also because she would be living here, indefinitely. She was in constant prayer about what lay ahead in the coming months. The ideas of new people, a new place, and new languages made her wary, but she was also thoroughly enjoying the adrenaline that was pumping through her body.

That feeling of excitement had been missing at the end of her first call back in southern New Jersey when she was still a parish pastor. Now these new faces were greeting her and the energy she felt sparked her creativity and her enthusiasm for furthering goals and responding to the needs of a community. When she had left her first call almost two years ago in 1989, she was drained empty and at the same time weighted down with feelings of failure, anger, and resentment. It had taken almost a year before she began to feel normal again. At the beginning of the year, she felt restless. She became more ready to go back to work, but even then, it wasn't at all clear what she wanted to do. She began working part-time and doing various ministries like teaching classes, filling in for other pastors who were away, and making herself busy. It didn't take long to grow tired of never having enough money. During that period of hiatus and "sabbatical" she had grown spiritually and began seeking guidance about what it was that God wanted from her. She didn't just want a job, but a mission, something meaningful; something where she could find genuine purpose and inspiration. Her experience had taught her some lessons about life, about faith, and about who she was. It wasn't all about the money, but Tanya was not going to give herself away anymore, not to men, or people or any cause. She was looking for fulfillment and to enjoy these next years of her life. She loved helping people, but she had learned the hard way how she could get caught up in the cycle of need and lose her way. Coming face to face with her own needs she had come to understand that meeting those needs was key to any support she could give to others. Sometimes it takes hard knocks to come to terms with concepts that should be easily understood.

What would she find here in Africa? More than anything she hoped to find more meaning and purpose. With a clean slate, her story could continue. Maybe she would be happy here and maybe she wouldn't. It seemed like she was in the right place at the right time. She was drawn into this particular journey even though it had not been easy to leave New Jersey where her family and friends were. That was the hardest part of all of it. The intense tugging at her soul made it possible for her to leave— even essential for her to leave what she knew and seek a new life. All of her crutches and excuses were back in New Jersey. She had the opportunity, the open door in front of her, and a new environment without expectations or preconceived notions to cloud her way.

* * * * * * * * *

Seven years before in 1982, long before Tanya's plane touched down in Yaoundé, she had dreams about houses. God's house was one, *The church where she became involved in her hometown in north Jersey was a structure that loomed between two fairly tall buildings -one a magnificent ionic Greek structure that had become the church's parish hall and the other an apartment building with 80 apartments in it. Because of this precarious location and the fact that the stained-glass windows were on the right and left sides of the church sanctuary, there was never much natural light in the church. Even with the lights on it was never very bright. But in the dream, the church was filled with the light of day. It was as if there was bright sunlight streaming into the sanctuary somehow. Tanya was leaving the building and as she looked back there was a strong breeze that swept through the church. It unsettled papers that were lifted and swirled around. It felt like the crisp outdoors after a rain shower when summer was just turning to autumn. Tanya looked back and saw the light and the wind. She went home. Then she heard a knock on the door.*

Tanya woke from her dream. Someone was knocking at the door. It was dark and she looked at the clock on her night table. It was 3 o'clock in the morning. She placed her hand on her husband's shoulder and gently shook him.

"Abdula! Someone is at the door. Abdula! Someone is knocking."

"Huh, what?" He was groggy, looking at her, squinting as she turned on the lamp.

"Someone is at the door."

"Ain't nobody knocking." He started to resume his snuggly position.

"Yes! There is someone there! I heard someone knocking."

Abdula got up, reluctantly, and went to the apartment door.

"Who is it?" He paused. "Who is it?" He opened the door and peeped out. "Ain't nobody there." He started back to the bedroom.

"I could have sworn I heard somebody knock on that door." Tanya switched off the lamp and scooted down under the covers.

"You know they say if you hear somebody knocking on your door and you don't see nobody there, it was either God or the devil," Abdula said as he rolled over.

Tanya bolted upright again. Now she remembered the dream! "Abdula, wait a minute. I was dreaming about church!"

She never forgot that night, because she found out from her pastors and spiritual mentors that the symbols in her dream had archetypal meanings, such as ancient and biblical implications, according to one pastor. The *wind* in the sanctuary, for instance, was symbolic of the *Spirit of God*, **ruah,** from the creation story, in Genesis. The wind is always a symbol of the Holy Spirit. Accordingly, the *light* of day in the generally darkened sanctuary is a symbol of the *light of Christ*, Jesus, the light of the world. *Water*, that fresh rain, was symbolic of baptism. She was excited by the interpretations as the calling stirred in her, so she pursued these ideas with her mentors, and she was clearly aware that she had not chosen this as a path forward. A career in ministry as she began to envision it was the strangest thing she had ever encountered.

After some meetings with the bishop's staff and the Candidacy Committee, arranged by her pastor, it was only a few months before she was enrolling in the fall semester of her first year at seminary in pursuit of a Master of Divinity degree. She probably should have had a place to live in Philadelphia before she did that. Abdula probably should have had a job in town, but he didn't. The house would present itself at the last minute before they had to end their search and plan a second search on another weekend. Eventually, Abdulla would be hired in a local school system. It was all worked out, and they felt affirmed.

Her academic journey comprised of three years of courses, one year of internship at a church, and a 10-week unit of chaplaincy at an institution, in her case, a hospital. She surprised herself and her teachers that she did so well. She relished soaking up all the learning she could to prepare herself for effective ministry. When she graduated, she was called and ordained to serve a small church in Chatsworth, NJ. This made sense because it was the same city where Abdula had found a teaching job. It was her pleasure to be a Black woman pastor in a Black church. She was one of a relatively small number of African American female pastors in her denomination nationwide and one of only five in the state of New Jersey. The black inner city church she was serving was unique in a denomination that was overwhelmingly white and middle-class.

Her task was to "re-develop" a dying congregation in a poor neighborhood, and she was up for the challenge when she got there—she was full of ideas and enthusiasm. Abdula was supportive, through the whole process, and he worked to finish his own Ph.D. program while teaching at the local high school. By the time she was ordained, he had published one book and was working on another. Back then everything seemed doable, even desirable.

****

The day that Tanya and Abdula moved into their home in the Woodside section of Chatsworth there was a parade. The two-story house they rented was on Brentwood Boulevard, a wide street in a neighborhood that had a history of affluence dating back to a time when there had been a large, successful Jewish population in the city. Two rapidly deteriorating stone columns still stood at the end of their block, as a monument to the idea that you had just arrived in the most prestigious section of Chatsworth. Here the traffic in one direction was distinctly separated from the traffic traveling in the other direction by the wide island in the middle of Brentwood Boulevard. The progression of time and social change had taken its toll on the scenario. The island that at one time had been perfectly manicured was now mostly sand, a dusty and trampled-upon strip. The ornate gates that at one time accompanied the columns were gone, and instead, young black men stood watch there, as was the case on so many of the corners throughout Chatsworth. Around the city the *open-air* sale of drugs was common. The landscape had certainly changed over the years, as had the population. Even so, the homes in this Woodside section of Chatsworth were bigger than those in other parts of the city. Many of the most gainfully employed residents lived in Woodside, some parts of which were still visibly upscale.

It made sense that the Fourth of July parade would march on Brentwood Boulevard which sloped down from the high school field where the parade started. Many things in Woodside originated at the *"Castle on the Hill"*, as Chatsworth

High School was affectionately called. Just the fact that Abdula taught there gained them a great deal of respect from the movers and shakers in town. Not to mention he was one of the best teachers they had. All the old-timers had graduated from that high school, and their children and now their grandchildren were coming through there. They were glad that Tanya and Abdula were sending their daughter, Mia, to school in Chatsworth. And Mia would attend the *Castle on the Hill.*

The prestige of bygone years, the glory of sports victories, homecomings, and many other historical high points were associated with the majestic-looking Chatsworth High School. Tanya would come to know that it was typical Chatsworth culture that important things began and ended in the Woodside neighborhood.

Tanya was excited about their new house and being done with seminary. She was excited about being newly ordained as a minister and about the call to pastor New Creation Church. This was exactly what she wanted to be doing, inner city ministry. She wanted to be immersed in it and to be daily engaged in the struggle of the community, contributing to it, walking hand in hand with the members of her church and her community.

Young girls of various shades of brown all dressed up in red and gold short skirts with double-breasted jackets that had golden tassels bouncing and swinging on them, were kicking up their legs, bodies gyrating, skillfully stomping and dancing, in their white three-quarter boots. The marching band played behind them dressed in matching uniforms as the extravaganza made its way up the boulevard. The horns blared and the drums kept the hard, pulsating beat. Tanya was overjoyed.

"This is great," Tanya exclaimed. She smiled and turned to a woman next to her. "Do they do this parade every year?"

The brown-skinned woman nodded, nonchalantly, as she hoisted her chubby toddler up on her hip. She looked Tanya up and down. "You just moved here?" she asked Tanya.

"Yes, I did." She pointed. "The third house in."

"Why?"

"Excuse me?" Tanya stopped clapping and rocking to the beat and looked at the woman more closely.

"Why? Why did you move here?" the woman asked.

"Oh…I just took a call at a church in town. I am a minister. My name is Tanya. How are you?"

"My name is Daisy, nice to meet you. So…you a minister?" She nodded her head and smiled. "You was **called** here by God…'cause I was gonna say…I know it must be something like that because nobody is just going to move to Chatsworth. You was called, by God!"

Tanya said. "I guess you don't like it here?"

"Nah…uh. I am trying my best *to get out* of Chatsworth! Nobody is trying to move *to* Chatsworth. Um-umph! Trying to move *from* Chatsworth!" She repeated herself, chuckling as she turned to leave.

Chatsworth was a city of neighborhoods, and Marsh, the neighborhood where New Creation Church was located was just 10 blocks from Tanya and Abdula's home. It was in the valley and every time it rained hard the area was sure to be flooded. If it was raining heavily Tanya would not be able to even get to church directly by car. She would have to find a circuitous route around the flood waters or risk stalling her car. The Marsh section had declined rapidly and steadily from a middle-class Polish neighborhood to a mostly Black and working-class neighborhood of homeowners and now, to a largely unemployed and transient, renting community. In Marsh, there were almost as many abandoned buildings as there were inhabited ones. Drugs, alcohol, teenage pregnancy, violence, and crime were more exaggerated in Marsh than anywhere else in the city.

Behind the church was a densely populated housing development, known as "the projects". The neighborhood was teeming with children and boasted no playgrounds and no libraries. Marsh schools were overcrowded. The maladies did not deter Tanya from her vision of a relevant church and the impact it could have on this community. She was determined and inspired. She made up brochures and leafleted the neighborhood. She started in July, and it was late for a summer program at Vacation Bible School, but she organized one anyway. She felt it was the best way to get to know families and to become highly visible. With those initial contacts, she built up a Sunday school and boosted church attendance for that fall. When Tanya came to New Creation there were only about 10 faithful members at the church who believed they couldn't be a church without a pastor. Tanya realized right away that she needed to bring in more members and more energy to build a viable congregation and ministry.

People in Chatsworth had no idea how good they had it. Tanya had just spent a month touring in Southern Africa with a group of newly formed religious leaders. Their delegation had witnessed many situations where black families lived in shanty towns and cooked with coal and in many cases didn't have running water or adequate sanitation. She had seen meat hanging from hooks being sold out of makeshift wooden booths while nearby raw sewerage ran through trenches dug into the ground alongside the road. In South Africa, black people got up in the dark and traveled by bus many miles to work in the more affluent towns doing menial jobs for little money. Worse than that, some families suffered because parents had to live where they worked for their white employers, in domestic situations or in corporate-run hostels and these workers rarely got to spend any time with their spouses and children, because their families lived in the "black only" homelands elsewhere. Black families in South Africa had to cope with the effects of years of an oppressive system of apartheid.

Tanya had been changed and inspired by her experience in South Africa. The black Christians she had met and stayed with there had managed to sing and praise God, dance and share, and be welcoming to a mixed group of Americans despite their own extreme circumstances. Tanya arrived in Chatsworth believing that the inner-city communities in America could overcome the problems they faced because they were much better equipped economically and socially. From her viewpoint, their situations did not seem insurmountable. She could see that in America there were many systems and resources that people simply took for granted.

Tanya walked the Marsh neighborhood every day positive in her presentation and outlook for what could happen for children and families there. She was creative and encouraged her church community and the community around the church. She worked with the people to organize street fairs and block parties, visited the projects, and showed up at people's doors with her flyers and brochures inviting them to church and bible study and meetings. She got down in the dirt on her hands and knees and planted marigolds and begonias in the front yard of the church.

20 | JOBETH

"Pastor Tanya, I don't know why you're planting them flowers down there. By tomorrow they won't even be there. The kids just gonna mess 'em up." Mary, one of her church members, stood on the sidewalk shaking her head at her from the other side of the fence.

"I don't know why you're saying that. I think they look nice." Tanya responded.

"They do look nice. But these people around here don't care about nothing like that." Mary said.

"Now Mary! That is the wrong attitude. Maybe if we care then other people might care too," Tanya said.

"You just so good-hearted, you crazy. And you better be careful going up in them projects. People be saying, 'I see your pastor everywhere'. You don't be scared?" Mary asked her.

"I guess I don't have sense enough to be scared." They both laughed.

Just then Jason, a kindly man who lived across the street came over. Tanya got up off her knees and greeted him as she brushed soil off of her jeans.

"Come here, Pastor Tanya." He led her over to her Mercury Sable hatchback that was parked on the street in front of the church. He pointed to the tail end of the car. "You know you got a bullet hole in your car?"

Tanya was shocked. "No! Is that what that is?" Then she remembered. She had been driving downtown a couple of days before and thought she heard a knock in the back of the car. At the time she thought she had driven over something on the street or that something had hit the car. There were a lot of abandoned buildings and empty lots in the section she was passing through. She did not see anyone or anything, so she kept going. Now she thought it was a good thing that she hadn't decided to stop and get out of her car to investigate what hit the car. She was in a hurry to take care of some business downtown and she had quickly forgotten about it until Jason showed her the tell-tale hole. Now she realized that there was danger all around her. A shiver ran through her just then and she sent up a prayer that God would continue to put a fence around her always and bless her and her ministry.

Tanya was a good preacher and a good organizer. She went through several phases of ministry in her 4 years at New Creation. When there was a massive fire that burned out 5 homes in the neighborhood, the church became the trauma center and the collection point for donations to help the families. Her ministry and her message went beyond "pie in the sky" as she encouraged her congregation to address the needs of the community. If Woodside was the most stable neighborhood and the best organized, then Marsh was the 'forgotten' neighborhood. The work with the fire crisis led to a working relationship with the Red Cross and a series of antiviolence programs for youth. During the time Tanya was pastor at New Creation, she led her church to become involved in community organizing and to create anti-drug campaigns, food ministries and to advocate for children and families. The church became well known as a safe haven for afterschool programs, and support groups that were positive for the community.

* * * * * * * * *

One of the ongoing challenges was an identity struggle that Tanya was confronted with on a personal and public level.

Chatsworth was its own little world, a small city made up of minorities, mostly Black and Puerto Rican. Mainline, traditionally white churches had to transition with the civil rights movement and white flight out of urban centers in the 60's and 70's. If these churches were to survive in neighborhoods that had changed culturally and ethnically, they had to reach out to a changed community and adapt their traditional style and music to the circumstances around them and New Creation was no different. Her church had even more to overcome because as a denomination in the Black community, they were more obscure than most. She was not Baptist and her denomination had been slow to embrace the changing environment over the years. The expectation that white leadership and paternalism would work in ethnic neighborhoods was experienced as a hostile presence within the Black community. On top of that, when more progressive leaders were brought in it was still not all that appealing to Black and Latinos who were more likely to be Baptist and Pentecostal in their backgrounds.

Tanya had her own reservations about her church denomination because of the cultural differences from her own Baptist upbringing. However, she was impressed with the grace-filled perspective of the faith practice and the social service that was evident to her. She related to a spiritual fervor that created a passion for social ministry. This was representative of Jesus Christ's mission of saving the world. Her experience of church during this time had introduced her to Jesus in a way that she had not experienced earlier in her younger years. The mission seemed to be truly focused on doing what Jesus did by being like Him, genuinely gracious and merciful. Tanya's experience in the more fundamentalist churches of her childhood was of a judgmental God who was unapproachable and negative and a church that was unapproachable and irrelevant.

She had stopped going to church as a teenager and while she felt a spiritual need she didn't feel spiritually alive or connected until the summer she was approached by a white pastor and asked to teach a summer program at a local Church in her neighborhood. That church was engaged in the community and the bible study, worship, and teaching opened the scriptures for her, so that she came to a different understanding of Jesus, as more inspiring and loving.

Tanya was actually ashamed of her sexual past which was influenced by her disconnection with any real moral guidance that made sense to her. Growing up in the perfect storm of the sexual revolution Tanya enjoyed "free love" and it seemed everybody was doing it. Her sexual practice was promiscuous and reckless. She was desperate to escape the intrusion of incest into her childhood. There was a malaise of confusion, ignorance, and shame in her makeup. She was making decisions, pretending, and withholding secrets before she could think straight. In her flight to stave off unwanted attention she chose to become sexually active with a partner of her choice who became protection in a sense. She was pregnant with Mia at the age of sixteen. Her own self-interest in youth ministry was an inspiration to others in the neighborhood. The children were drawn to ministry programs that were designed for them.

During her first Christmas season with the church, she experienced the story of Mary mother of Jesus, and her pregnancy, her youth, and the feeling of fear and uncertainty in a way that was personal and relatable. The community she had stumbled on was loving and they made the faith very personal for people. Tanya liked that and she saw that the church was concerned with helping and had schools and programs and camps that would be good for her daughter. The church was a big help for her as a single parent. Mia's father served his purpose in her life but succumbing to drug addiction it was clear he was not going to be in the picture going forward. Tanya accepted that she had made a mistake, but she decided she would manage. She took advantage of every opportunity to improve and educate herself.

Mia was young enough to relate to Abdula as her father after they got together. Tanya was pleased that her husband was happy to adopt Mia as his own. They settled into a comfortable workable family life. The seminary community they moved into was a nurturing one for Tanya and Mia. There was a throng of seminary children who attended the small elementary school near the campus. This made it easy to bring Mia through the seminary episode of their life.

Tanya embraced the idea that there were likely hundreds of drifting souls who just like her wanted a spiritual connection but didn't have one. She knew there were other people who were turned off from church for whatever reasons and who could be helped by meeting the kind of Jesus she had found. Tanya would challenge the wider church to go further in reaching out as a church to become more diverse, and to be changed *within* by persons of color and language. It was hard for her to go to regional and national gatherings and see how white the church was. It was a war of the worlds to go between the churches like those in Chatsworth, Newark, North Philadelphia, and Chicago and the typical churches of white suburbia and most of the Midwestern United States. The mainstream denomination of which she was a part, was doing some marvelous work, but it was still very white.

As Tanya began doing ministry she did not have to pay too much attention to the larger church as she was focused on putting together services and practicing relevant ministry on the ground in Chatsworth. At New Creation, they had "testimony time" and gospel music and altar call. These were not typical practices across her denomination, but at New Creation, she knew they needed to appeal to the culture of the community they served. It was fun to be doing what she felt was exciting ministry. She was 'new' enough and naïve enough to be bold about tweaking the liturgy and practices of the church. New Creation would host prayer breakfasts and have revivals. Their practices were often questioned by visitors from sister churches, but Tanya felt it was justified because she was trying to reach people who needed to meet Jesus. People who had been overlooked by her church. She knew the church was a platform on which reformation had been built before. The faith could be translated into the language of the people.

Tanya pulled out the stops any way that she could. The church had a bell tower and the children would swing on the thick ropes as the weight of the bell pulled them up. She imagined that riding would stay in their memory forever. Children were very attracted to the church, and they brought life and their families.

Mary, who had become a faithful member of the church, was wrong about people not caring because people did care. When Tanya met Mary, she was strung out on drugs, and she wanted to get clean. She became involved in church with her children, and then got into a drug treatment program and got herself cleaned up. Mary like so many people in Chatsworth, wanted more than anything to live a better life. It just wasn't easy to achieve when there was so much negativity and ugliness all around. Tanya and the whole community struggled every day to overcome the depressed, chaotic atmosphere they lived in.

Mary was wrong, but there was some truth in what she said. Some people made it, and some didn't. Some sought escape like the woman on the parade route. Many people succeeded in getting out of Chatsworth. Some people just succumbed and were pulled into poverty despair and dysfunction. Mary testified many times how Pastor Tanya and her church family had saved her from drowning in it all. So many people found themselves drowning in a bottle or beaming up on crack or some other mind-numbing substance. A few, like Mary, somehow survived and overcame and managed to find their way back to some semblance of a decent life. Some people found ways to compensate and desperate ways to survive. That was what happened to Pastor Tanya when she started to sink; she found her own rather desperate ways to survive.

* * * * * * * * *

PART TWO

Blessed Are The Poor

One Sunday morning Tanya was in the church long before anyone else arrived when she heard a man's voice call out to her from the doorway. She recognized him as a man who was not a churchgoer, but she knew his family. She had ministered to his mother when his father passed away.

"Pastor Tanya, good morning. I'm Jake – Mavis' son."

"Yes, I recognize you." She was glad he had reminded her of his name and greeted him with a handshake.

Jake didn't look too clean. He looked as if he had been hanging out all night. He was being deliberately respectful toward her, casting his eyes downward while he held his baseball cap in his hand."

"What can I do for you Jake?" she asked.

"I want to ask you to visit my mother. They found my sister dead this morning. They don't know what happened. I just thought you could go by there and see my mother."

"Of course…of course. I am so sorry to hear that. You say they don't know what happened?" She asked. "And how are you? You want to sit down?"

His hand was already on the doorknob. "No, no. I'm okay. I just want you to see my mother." A tear rolled down his bony dark face. Tanya reached out and gently patted him on his back.

"I am truly sorry to hear this about Doris. She had a child didn't she?"

"Yeah, two. They are with my mom…just please, go see my mom."

"I will Jake. If you need anything…" He was gone and Tanya just sat down on the staircase and cried. It was like that. She did the funeral. She did the funeral for Jake's sister and so many others. She did a lot of funerals for people who weren't members of New Creation. She felt she was not just the pastor of the church members but a pastor of the community as well.

At home, she and Abdula were struggling. They both gave a lot to others…Abdula as a teacher, writer, and activist, and Tanya as a pastor and community activist. They were out more than they were in; apart more than they were together. They were living their dreams, but as time passed Tanya was running out of steam. She came home exhausted and just wanted someone to care for her. Too often Abdula was just not there even when he was there. It became clear that Abdula was not only addicted to his work, but he was addicted to excess in other ways too. He was drinking too much, and he had other women.

Tanya blamed herself for some of it. She had looked for ways to placate herself when Abdula was not able to be there for her and began to flirt with other men. Some men found her vivacious personality and her passion attractive. In her mind, her neediness and loneliness justified her crossing the boundaries of her situation. Both Tanya and Abdula often went away to conferences and traveled a fair amount in connection with their professional and political obligations. They claimed to have no trust issues between them at first, but in fact, they did, because neither of them could be trusted.

Abdula was in his own exciting world that was deeply involved with the political and the theological. These concerns were intertwined with academia as he pursued his Ph.D. He taught, wrote. and traveled to meetings and cohorts. He was often gone for days at a time. Once he did not return home from an academic meeting that had started over drinks on a

Friday afternoon until Sunday afternoon. Tanya did not hear from Abdula all this time. She felt disregarded and forgotten. Abdula would leave town and be gone for several days in New York. Tanya felt that he and his religious leaders were trying to save the world whenever they got together.

Tanya was increasingly needy, more socially and emotionally than sexually. She was emotionally drained, looking for replenishment and it seemed sex could provide some comfort or distraction. Maybe sex made her feel valued on some level. She had a promiscuous side that she generally had learned to hold at bay. But it was becoming more evident.

During, one summer vacation break, she traveled to a retreat in upstate New York. She took the train to relax and not have the stress of driving. It was a two-hour train ride, and when she met a Nigerian man on the way it triggered her sexually. Tanya was always intrigued by men with accents. She was sitting in the row just in front of him. She knew she was a goner as soon as she overheard him speak.

He was on his cell phone obviously talking to a woman and explaining how he had not had time to call her while he was at meetings in New York City, but he was on his way home and would call her that night. When he hung up, to Tanya's amazement, he called another woman, and when she answered, he asked her what she was wearing and if she missed him. He told her he couldn't wait to see her. Tanya was sitting in the seat in front of him and could not help overhearing his conversations.

When he hung up, she turned around to face him and said, "I can see why they would fall for that." She had to see what he looked like with that accent and sexy voice.

He laughed as he turned his attention to her, showing his perfect white teeth. He was the color of chestnuts, and he was thick. She liked big men. He was dressed impeccably in a brown suit, a tan dress shirt, and a tie. He threw his head back still smiling and spoke. "I am so embarrassed."

"Oh, you're embarrassed! You are embarrassed because you are a player?" She was clearly flirting with him. He seemed good-natured.

"I guess I got caught." They both laughed.

"Mind if I sit with you?" He queried.

"I don't mind at all."

Soon, they were talking about the business meetings he was coming from and the retreat she was going to. They were attracted to one another. Tanya had no idea what happened to the woman he was going to call that night. She felt sorry for her for about one minute because he spent the night with Tanya in her hotel room. True, she barely knew him, but she had opportunity and motive and she felt she had better strike while it was hot.

Abdula was not taking care of business at home with Tanya, but after 6 years, he knew his wife. He suspected right away that she had a boyfriend. The truth of the matter was she didn't. In fact, Tanya was just sleeping around a bit. Sex as a release was even more exciting with someone new. She got to where she could not remember the last time she and Abdula had had sex. Her church denomination was a national corporation and that meant they had meetings all over the country and she had colleagues in every state. Sometimes lay people just don't realize what life is like for a lot of religious leaders. In fact, it is stressful, and it is neurotic and draining. When the pastors get together away from home, despite the holy nature of their business, there is a fair amount of drinking and sexualizing that can go on.

Tanya didn't drink much, but she was certainly not above getting laid. In fact, certain things about the ministry made her horny as hell. For instance, in the early years Abdula knew that on Sunday afternoons after preaching, the only thing that Tanya wanted to do besides sleep was to make love. He had accommodated her. Lately, the spark that ignited them was missing.

There were a lot of highly charged situations in the ministry. Nothing got her libido going quite like a visit to the intensive care ward or having to meet a whole family screaming and crying in the emergency room because their loved one was shot in the back on the corner. There was something about allowing herself to be available to trauma that caused a stirring up of excitement and emotions. Often pain, fear, and waves of failure were emotions experienced in the emergency room, intensive care, and at the bedside of the dying. So maybe it wasn't the best idea to get it on with the resident hospital chaplain, but he was so cute, and he was also totally stressed out.

By the time Abdula and Tanya got divorced, it was just a formality. They were not having sex anymore, at least not with each other, and they argued constantly about broken promises and the ways that they chose to get back at each other. They both accepted that it was time. It was hard for the people around them because they were so well respected, as a couple. Most people saw them as a shining example of respectable black marriage even if that was far from the truth. The breakup took its toll on her and their daughter, Mia, too. Tanya probably should have left the church when she broke up with Abdula, but there was a part of her that could not lose anything else just then. Her life was changing drastically, and she didn't think she could handle so much change all at once.

Mia didn't do too well in school that year and Tanya accepted that their home life had affected her grades. Abdula and she had not considered the needs of others. Living in Chatsworth meant being in crisis mode most of the time and it often got down to self-preservation, when people did what they had to do to survive. For Tanya, part of it was about putting out this fire or that fire.

All of a sudden Abdula was gone and it wasn't too much longer before Mia was gone too -- off to college. Tanya felt she had lost her moorings somehow, and she was also extremely alone. She worked harder and working harder made her needier than ever. She met Richard Epps in the church basement. He was running a community meeting to which no one had shown up. They were both needy at the moment.

Things stayed intense, professionally, as well as with the intensity that characterized her relationship with Richard. Tanya was less and less able to keep up, after a while, with the demands of the ministry. The neighborhood continued to decline. The incidence of violence went unabated. After five years Tanya felt like there was no real joy in her work anymore. Her relationship with Richard was unhealthy because he had an abusive personality, and she was simply hanging on to him because she was living in a world where she felt she didn't have anyone who was truly a friend. She was sleeping with Richard, so he seemed like the closest thing to a friend she had. She was consumed with regret and professionally, she just wasn't trying hard anymore.

The leadership at the church was unsteady. People kept moving away and many of the ones who stayed were either over-dependent or disillusioned. Tanya found, in the end, that she was gasping for air. She was having inappropriate relationships as she sought to get away from Richard. Of course, she was making very bad choices based on sexual intrigue and that behavior just made her feel worse. The worst thing about it was that she kept winding up back with Richard who just loved to harp on her weaknesses. When she could not imagine meeting the challenges in front of her anymore, she resigned her call at the church.

* * * * * * * * *

On one of the coldest days in the northeastern United States in two years, Tanya pulled her sweater cap down over her dreadlocks and further down over her forehead, as she walked. Her face still stinging, she sniffed and wanted to get the tissue out of her bag, but it was too cold to do anything except brace against the harsh wind. Along these blocks near the city line of Chatsworth, there were no tall buildings to break the wind that blew off the river across the sparse landscape. One side of the street was dominated by a large parking lot sprawling out in front of a major supermarket. Across the expanse of Newton Avenue, there was parking space in front of a strip of sundry discount stores and a McDonald's restaurant that now occupied the space old-timers fondly remembered as the location of the old drive-in theater that once was. Tanya entered the small savings bank and saw that the one customer service clerk was seated at a desk talking to a couple, so she sat down in the waiting area. There were only a few people on the lines in front of the windows where two tellers handled business. She was glad for the time to wait, so she could blow her nose and wipe away the tears that were freezing on her face…time for the feeling in her fingers to return. She told herself to look like everything was okay. After about fifteen minutes the

Asian clerk finished with the couple and nodded at Tanya to approach the desk. The woman with the round olive face smiled at her.

"How can I help you?"

"I'd like to open up a checking account." The dark-haired woman motioned for her to sit down and began asking her pertinent questions looking intently at the computer monitor, navigating the mouse, as she pecked at the keyboard. Tanya couldn't see the screen because of the angle. She looked around trying to act unconcerned about what came up on the woman's computer screen. The bank looked somewhat disheveled. A *boom box* radio sat on top of a file cabinet that was turned backwards. It was on loud enough to hear the oldies station it was tuned to. Tanya remembered working in a bank in New York City some years ago. She hated that job. That radio would not have been allowed in that crisp clean conservative atmosphere. But this was South Jersey, 20 years later; this was not where the big money was kept. Chatsworth was one of the poorest cities in the nation.

The woman asked for her social security number. Wasn't her Social Security number on the license Tanya had just given her? The license sat at the base of the clerk's keyboard while she entered data. Tanya said the numbers. This was a new bank for her. She had to open a checking account and she hoped she would be successful. *Just let one thing go right, she thought.* Her account at her former bank was overdrawn for a couple of months. They closed it. Is that little tidbit of information going to pop up on the screen and cause a problem? She felt so helpless, but she had to try. Money talks, as they say. She was opening the account with $600.00, a child support check.

Tanya blew her nose. The tears that kept coming could have been from the cold or something else. She had walked the two long blocks past the shopping center, and she would walk the same blocks back to the employment office. Across the street from the employment office, there was a diner. Chatsworth had one diner and one supermarket, which meant you couldn't avoid people you knew. Tanya just wanted to hide. To hide her unemployment…to hide her financial messes…to hide the fact that she had quit her job after 5 years.

"Hi, how are you?"

"I'm fine. How about you?" She had a beautiful smile and she felt obligated to be "blessed", that is not to complain. Everything had to be all right. People expected the pastor to be blessed.

At least she was up and out today which was an accomplishment. Today was busy as she was determined to move her situation forward. While she waited her turn at the bank, she reflected on her first stop that day which had been the community center. She knew one of the coordinators employed there from when she worked with him in a community organizing effort while she was still pastor at New Creation Church. He had told her the last time she called him that when he knew something, he would tell her. She suspected he might be annoyed with her after she called him several times. But she *had* to go there again. He couldn't call her if her phone wasn't working. She was going to ask again. Either there was a job or there was not. Let him be annoyed.

Actually, she found Emmanuel relaxed and pleasant when the receptionist informed him Tanya was there to see him. He smiled cheerfully as he ran down the stairs with open arms.

38 | JOBETH

He hugged her, invited her into the kitchen, and offered her a chair.

"Truthfully, it's kind of hard right now because it is the end of our fiscal year. We are budgeting and getting a lot of things in order." Emmanuel was a very good-looking Puerto Rican. He was suave and about 15 years her junior.

"Have some coffee, Pastor Tanya."

"No, thank you." She declined.

"How about a cup of tea?" Tanya declined his second offer, and he went on to explain that he thought the center would have some staff needs soon because they had recently lost some people.

A few minutes into their conversation a dark-haired white woman came down the stairs. Emmanuel called to the woman who looked to be about 22 years old and introduced her as Candy, the Site Director. He told the woman that Tanya was a minister with a lot of experience working with youth in the community. The woman seemed interested, and Tanya wasted no time getting a resume into her hand.

Candy looked at the resume thoughtfully and said, "In fact, we do need chaperones to work with the afterschool program because we are so shorthanded and whenever anyone calls out, we really get jammed. Why don't we have you fill out an application? It's not much, and you will have to help out with classes…if you're interested…?"

"I'm interested. I need a full-time job but it's something. You say…chaperone?"

"Yes," Candy explained. "You would have to meet the kids at the school and ride the school bus with them to the site."

Emmanuel said. "Let me get you an application." Then apologetically, "I am sorry I didn't tell you about this before." Tanya understood he was not the person in the position of calling the shots. But he was her initial contact. She also understood that he and so many other people just didn't understand how badly she needed money. Not having a car made it very difficult, so the fact that the two schools Candy mentioned were within walking distance from her house was workable. She could do this…finally, something she could do, that she wouldn't mind doing.

Now as she sat at the bank clerk's desk, the calendar on the desk reminded her that the date was the 24th of January 1990. She was glad she had remembered that something did go in the right direction at the community center. Something was better than nothing. One, two, three, four…ten days. In ten days, she was to go to court in response to the eviction notice her landlord had served her. She didn't like thinking about what would happen after that. She would be as bad off as the worst stories she had seen on the news the night before: *A woman with four children tried to keep her children warm through the night when her husband had died earlier in the week. He was a minister too, and he bought a house because he knew he was sick. He wanted to provide for his family, but he didn't live to get the house ready. He died. The house was cold. And in other news… the region has been declared "code blue". It was cold. A church opened its doors to the homeless. The minister of the church said if you didn't have a place to go you could come there that night.*

Well, apparently no bad news showed up on the bank computer. The woman explained her new checking account and informed her that the cash would not be available to her until the following Tuesday. She had $4.00 in her pocket, and it was Thursday. But still, she could breathe a sigh of relief because she needed to have an account. She had no way to handle a check. Just that was a small amount of legitimacy. Something would be in order. She was feeling low on order these days. The cell phone was shut off. She tried to call a colleague that morning and could not get the call through. She had expected her service to be discontinued several days before, and finally, time had run out. It would be hard to find a job without a phone.

She walked back to the diner. Earlier she had called her friend, Liz from the payphone, to see if she could cash her child support check for her. Tanya had explained that her account had been closed, but Liz had said she was not in a position to help her. That's when Tanya decided to go ahead and risk embarrassment and rejection by trying to open a new checking account.

"Oh, Tanya, things are getting desperate for you." Liz sounded worried for her.

"I am trying not to go crazy with it all. You can't call me Liz…they shut my phone off this morning." She made an attempt at sounding upbeat. "What are you doing tonight? I am going to the Christian Unity service at Bethany…are you busy?"

What did she have…the church and her need for God's grace and the comfort of her faith?

"No, I can't go…that's too bad. I would love to go, but I've got meetings tonight." Liz moaned on the other end of the phone.

"Oh, okay…well, I have to go. I'll call you soon. Bye now."

Tanya dialed the Homeless Coalition when she hung up from Liz. Just following up on a meeting she had there the week before with the Director. They had talked about the possibility of her taking a job as a receptionist. If she could have had a case manager job that would be better, but without a car, that was impossible. The HR Director told her she could probably get her started by next Thursday.

"They cut my phone off. I will call you, and I am going to find out how to get there by public transportation."

"Great. Ask Lucy at the Chatsworth site about the buses, she would know. When you come just tell them at the desk to let me know you are here." This older Black woman seemed to understand what was happening in Tanya's life and that she needed to get a job quickly. She had skills, which she hoped were at least marketable. At least she had a bus pass. With the pass, even when she didn't have much money, she could still get around.

Now as she fished for change in her handbag near the diner entrance again, an acquaintance who had seen her there earlier in the vestibule hanging around the phone booth came out of the restaurant.

"Are you alright?" He looked surprised to see her again.

"Oh, I am fine. She replied with a big smile. "I have an appointment across the street but it's too early." He accepted that and left. She knew he would have given her a ride if she had asked. She was so ashamed. Her condition was a secret.

She needed change for the phone. This was a good place to make phone calls; it was inside and out of the cold. She went in and ordered a cup of coffee and a Danish. She needed something in her stomach and to get 50 cents in coins. Now she would have 75 cents left. She hoped she would be able to reach someone she considered a friend, on the phone. Bonnie answered when she reached her at the principal's office of her small alternative school. They planned to go to the bishop's council meeting together on Saturday morning.

Tanya invited her to church that evening, but Bonnie had choir practice.

Bonnie said, "Get your phone back on, lady!"

Tanya laughed, "Yeah with what money? They are not going to turn it back on because I want them too." People are nice but they didn't know what this was like. How could they? She hadn't known until now. Soon she might be homeless and it was very cold outside. She sipped her coffee, ate her Danish, and then bundled herself up to go over to the employment office. The change jingled in her pocket as she ran across the street. She didn't even stop to smoke the one cigarette she had left. It was too cold to be standing outside. She went in and registered.

Tanya sat through the orientation to the employment service program and then was taken to see an interviewer. The woman was good at her job and reminded Tanya that her marketable skill was in the area of social service. She discussed things Tanya could do and how to go about it. The interviewer also gave her some advice about her resume.

Whenever Tanya could get excited, and muster up some hope, things seemed better. A positive productive day was good for that. The employment service allowed her access to computers and the Internet anytime she wanted. She could use email, which meant at least she had a form of communication with some of her contacts. Tanya had been a pastor full-time for 5 years. Before that, she was in seminary for 4 years. It had been a long time since she had been in an employment office... a long time since she had had to look for a job. It was a vulnerable, miserable place she found herself in, and she did not have a whole lot of confidence.

That evening she put on her clerical robes for the first time in a month and a half. She had been looking forward to this

Christian Unity service. Many churches participated through the week with services held at different churches, hosted by different denominations each night. She was glad to see some pastors she was accustomed to working with as well as lay people from various churches around the city that she had not seen for a while. People greeted her warmly. It was comfortable to be in the role she knew so well. The service was good. She wasn't in charge, but she knew what to do in this setting. She led prayers and enjoyed the service. She did not let on that she had 75 cents to her name. She would get by. It had been a successful day, all things relative. Her faith said God doesn't come when you want but was always on time. She had to believe that, even though it seemed bleak at times…she had to believe things were going to work out in a miraculous way. It had been a year of struggle and she wasn't homeless yet. The last song they sang that night was **We Shall Overcome.**

She was acutely aware she had not been down this particular road before. Life is a kind of journey, and you know where you've been before, even if you've forgotten. It is a feeling you get. The feeling she got just then was a low burning in the bottom region of her belly and she suspected it was fear. For all her strength and her faith, she knew she was teeter-tottering on the edge of life, maybe the edge of sanity.

****

James died. James was a recovering heroin addict. He had struggled in life and managed to find his way into a job with a good organization that helped a lot of homeless people. Through helping other people, he had found a measure of dignity. As a Black man, he was a "nobody" by the standards of the world and in the minds of those who set the standards.

At the homeless shelter, he was appreciated for what he did, for the kindness he had shown, the bags he lifted, and the protection he offered to staff and volunteers in a sometimes harsh environment. He had always liked Tanya because she danced. She was the pastor who came to lead chapel for the guests and engaged the staff and the guests in *praise dance*. He appreciated that and respected her because she had found a way to break down a lot of the defenses of the rough crowd she walked into, by using music, dance, and charm. Tanya went to the funeral that day and for James, she danced to **Precious Lord**. She had been asked to read the gospel lesson, but she was moved to dance before she read it. She asked a woman who was a guest with a lovely voice to sing the familiar hymn. Tanya approached the podium and she said she wanted to add her testimony to all the others that had been given. She walked out into the aisle and as the words of the hymn rose into the air, she extended her arms over her head and did the dance in James' honor. When she was done, she went back to the podium and read the lesson.

She was drawn these days to the homeless shelter. The Upper Room which was a support facility for persons living with HIV/AIDS was also housed in the building. She wasn't always visiting the shelter to preach or to dance. Sometimes she came to get food for herself in those days. She would cut down on what she shopped for by getting food from the food pantry at the shelter. She also inquired at the Upper Room about employment. The more time she spent at the shelter, the more comfortable she felt. She thought of herself when she looked at the people who came to take a shower, to wash their clothes and just to get in out of the cold. How many weeks would pass by before she, herself, was in the same situation?

Saturday morning, she awakened to the incessant shrieking of the alarm clock, on a table near her window which forced her to have to get up to turn it off. It was 6:30 AM and she didn't want to but had to go to the Bishop's Council meeting that morning. She didn't want to hear twenty people ask her how she was or to have to answer them. She was still on the council even though she had not been in a pastoral office for seven months. She was not feeling good about the bishop and his staff because they had yet not found her a call. She wondered if they were even trying. If not, then why? She saw something white in her hair in the bathroom mirror after she got out of the shower, and when she tried to remove it, she realized it was her graying hair. When the check cleared, she was going to have to get some hair dye. She smiled at herself in the mirror. She was pretty and did not think of herself as old. Apparently, some other people did. The woman in the employment office told her not to put her high school information on her resume because employers might discriminate.

"Why, because of the city?"

"No, because of the year." That was a rude awakening for Tanya. She was 47 and to many people that was old.

"Well too bad, because I am still coming!" She said to her reflection in the mirror. She waved her hand in the air and snapped her fingers; then she brushed her teeth and finished getting dressed.

The meeting was long, but it wasn't as bad as she thought it would be. There were some topics on the agenda that interested her, and she was vocal in expressing her opinions and challenging some ideas. After lunch, the Secretary presented the nominating committee report. The committee needed two more nominations for statewide Secretary and one for Treasurer. They asked the council for nominations. Karen, a council member was impressed enough by Tanya to want to nominate her for Secretary. She kept looking at Tanya, motioning and lip-syncing an invitation, and Tanya kept shaking her head no.

When they took a break, Karen came over to her. "You ought to let me nominate you."

"Oh, no. That is a lot of work. Too much." Tanya rolled her eyes up in her head in an exaggerated gesture.

"You're up for it. You have the energy. I think you would be great. You heard them – you write your own job description." Karen was insistent.

"I don't know." Tanya had never thought about being an officer on the council. Now she was thinking about the political ramifications and the exposure. Maybe it might help her get a call. Maybe it wasn't such a bad idea. The problem was that she had no telephone, no car and it looked like she might not even have a home to live in. What kind of secretary could she be?

"I'll think about it." And she would. Nominations could still be made at the next meeting as well as from the floor of the assembly in May. Who knew where she would be down the line …maybe her situation would improve.

How many times has it been said that people in high places put their pants on the same way as everybody else? Even so, the Bishop, Rob Wilson could be the one holding her future in his hand. Of course, he asked her how she was doing.

"That's a hard question for me to answer these days."

He looked thoughtful. "I thought it was awfully brave of you to leave New Creation when you did." He seemed to imply that it wasn't wise to leave one job without the prospect of another on the horizon. He continued, "I understand the circumstances, but there is just not a whole lot to offer you right now." He reasoned that while there were many congregations without pastors, there were also many congregations that did not have the financial resources available to call a pastor. Have you been substituting for your colleagues regularly?"

"Not really." She answered. "Nobody's on vacation yet. I haven't been subbing a whole lot in the few months I have been on leave."

"Are you working?"

"No. I had to leave the little part-time job I had when I had my surgery. They didn't want me to, but I had to take some time off. I was back and forth to the hospital and doctors, and I had to take some recovery time. I may be starting a new job next week...it's been rough."

"I will speak to the office staff and make sure they give you priority for substitute jobs."

"Thank you, Rob." And she thought, "He is out of his mind!" She needed a few thousand such opportunities just to make things right, and he was talking about sub-jobs that paid less than $200.00 each. How much more could she take? Well, it wasn't over yet. she broached another issue.

"I read in the reports that St. Michael's is probably going to close."

"Yes." The bishop nodded. "There is no congregation there."

"Well, I don't mean to thwart the process...Maybe it needs to close. But what about a new mission there? I just feel that what was needed there, was never done. I was thinking about what would happen if we started all over again brand new. I would be willing to try some bold new initiatives there."

"That's a thought. A pastor and his wife from another congregation are living in the parsonage right now and that building has a lot of problems. If the parsonage were vacant, we could think about doing that. Right now, it is just a lot of upkeep…a lot of problems. But it's a thought." Oh well, she thought, she had said it, for whatever it was worth. She wanted to ask him for money, but she hated begging. She hated thinking that she needed him to be her "sugar daddy", although he had given her money in the past. Did that make it better or worse for her? She just couldn't take a rejection of her request for money at this moment. She was angry enough as it was. Maybe she would feel she had no choice but to ask later in the week.

He asked her about her health. "It was a relief to all of us when we got your message that your tests came back benign."

"And I appreciated knowing that everybody was praying for me. Prayer works. I am just fine…thank you for asking."

The breast cancer scare was an unforgettable ordeal. She had found several lumps in her left breast, which turned out to be cysts. They had been removed. On top of all the uncertainty about her future, she had faced the possibility of death. But she didn't die. It made her believe that there was something God still wanted her to do.

She remembered being wheeled into the operating room. It was so bare. It felt more like a slaughterhouse, although sterile. She hardly recognized Dr. Ramirez because her face was covered with a mask, and she had what looked like a shower cap on her head. Some attendants transferred her from the stretcher to the operating table. They extended two arms out from the table and fastened her arms to them.

She lay there with her arms stretched out on either side, at their mercy and she thought she knew how Jesus felt on the cross. She had to say it out loud even if it was a ridiculous statement. The anesthesiologist was sitting behind her on a stool, at her head, about to put her under with the mask he held in his hand. The last conscious moment in the operating room she heard him say, "At least you know He is here with you." And then it was dark. Time passed and when she woke up, she couldn't stop coughing and she couldn't stop crying.

She had even put in an application for employment while she was running back and forth to the hospital during that time. A minister who was in the position of Social Service Director at the hospital was about to resign. He had encouraged her to apply for his job.

* * * * * * * * *

Tanya was not only floundering professionally and financially, but also socially. Since the divorce from Abdula and her resignation from New Creation, her stress levels had decreased by a couple of levels, and she was not traveling regularly anymore. Her focus was more local, albeit the pickings were slim in Chatsworth and the immediate area. She wound up in a relationship with the local undertaker who along with his widowed mother was trying to keep a faltering funeral home afloat following the demise of the charismatic husband, father, and CEO. Richard, Sr., who was a mortician and businessman, was adept and successful as a funeral home director. His wife and son were not so skilled. The business had declined over the years. Somehow, Richard, Jr. had a hold on Tanya. For her, he was different and exciting. And he had a car and a job.

50 | JOBETH

"I don't like you having no telephone," Richard said as he came in her front door brushing past her into the living room of the two-story row home she was renting. He was a big man, although he hated when people called him 'Big Guy'.

"I am going to get you a phone."

"I don't like it either. It's kind of hard to look for a job when you don't even have a phone." Tanya said as she locked the door behind him.

"May I have some tea?" Richard asked as he sat down on the couch and picked up the remote for the television. Tanya went into the kitchen and put on some water to boil. Right now, she was very annoyed with Richard and their off-and-on relationship that never seemed to go anywhere. He was a personification of the rut she was in. He was a poor excuse for company at best. It would be nice if he got her a phone, but Tanya had learned over and over again that she could not depend on Richard.

One time he told her that he was going to give her a thousand dollars. At the time she was two months behind in her rent. He came over to her house and gave her $30.00.

"What is the matter?" He had asked her as she looked at him in disbelief.

"Didn't you tell me you were going to give me a thousand dollars?"

"I was just joking with you. Where am I going to get $1,000.00? You thought I was for real?"

"Yes, I thought you were for real! You know that I need the money! Why would you play with me like that? I am not making all this up!"

She knew she couldn't depend on Richard for anything. She brought him the tea.

Again, on Sunday Richard told her he was going to get her a phone.

"You keep saying that." She quipped.

"Well, I don't know how to go about it."

"Well, I know how." She said.

Tanya was still struggling financially, and she needed something to happen soon. She might have been further along, but her experience with the breast surgery was a major psycho-emotional setback. It was yet another occasion for Richard to demonstrate how he could not be there for her. He had mysteriously disappeared during that time.

Tanya was grateful to be healthy and alive because a month earlier she had been waiting for the results of a breast biopsy and recovering from surgery. Whatever happened she had to remember that as bad as things were, they could have been worse if her biopsy had been malignant.

The cancer scare had put her back in touch with her true friends and her family. It made her closer to God. It made her hopeful for the future. Her feelings about Richard had changed. She realized that she didn't *need* him in her life if he was not going to be a supportive presence. She began to feel emotionally distant from him like she was leaving him even when she was sitting right next to him. She did love him, in a certain way, and she would miss having sex with him, but she valued her life and purpose more now and she wasn't going to allow him to continue to hurt her. He was not her man even if he wanted to masquerade as such. Maybe there was a man for her in this world or maybe not. All of a sudden it wasn't as important as it once was. She had been using sex and men as her personal tool, her way to pacify herself and provide herself with a certain kind of release. Her focus was changing, and she was starting to find her way to a more wholesome and meaningful way of living. She was grateful for her health – physically and spiritually.

Tanya was able to get a prepaid phone when the check she deposited cleared. She brought it home and set it up to charge, leaving the box and the manual spread out on the kitchen table. On Wednesday evening Richard came by and when he saw the phone, he commented.

"Oh, yeah," she said. "I have something for you." She fished out the receipt from the pocket of her coat that hung on a wall hook. She handed it to him, and he looked at it. His eyes went wide and his dark, thick brows furrowed.

"A hundred and thirty-seven dollars!" He held out the receipt to hand it back to her. "I can't give you no hundred and thirty-seven dollars! I'll give you something toward it, but I can't pay for that." He was shaking his head.

"Fine. Richard, the phone is all paid for. Give me that." She took the receipt and put it back in her pocket. It was a test, and he had failed it. She had made him look bad and that didn't sit well with him. He was triggered into a tirade of name-calling and negative regard directed at her.

"Who do you think you are?" He asked her.

"Richard, I only gave you the receipt because you said you were going to get me a phone. You said it more than once."

"Yes. *I* was going to get you a phone!" He emphasized *"I".*

"Well, you also said you didn't know how to go about it. I just went and got it."

"Well, then you pay for it. They have phones for $49 in Philly. I'm not giving you shit." He just wouldn't let it go. He kept hollering and calling her a *bitch*. After about five minutes of this craziness, she asked him to please go home.

"I already know I can't depend on you Richard. That's why I just went and got the phone. You can go home now. I have a lot of things on my mind." She walked him to the door. "Good night."

There was a time when she would have argued with him and would have called him worse names than he called her. And they would have probably made passionate love. But those days were over. She got the phone because in order to find a job she had to be in touch with people. And she put him out because there was no point in him staying. She didn't need to argue with him. It was a strange feeling, falling out of love.

Her thinking was all wrong. She realized that later. When she first met Richard, she was a lonely divorcee who was unhappy and burnt out. Her relationship with him did have a payoff. It wasn't all bad. It was just that the price had become way too high. Being wanton, abusing herself, and someone else, was a high price to pay for a little pleasure. Richard was not good for her, and yet she kept seeing him. He lied to her. He disrespected her and he brought out the worst in her. She used him and he used her and when it was all over, she hated him, and she hated herself.

One thing she had done right in her profession of ministry is she generally kept up access to a therapist. She had marriage problems, interpersonal relationship issues and she sought retreat and some behavioral health support that was available to her. Her denomination included psychological testing and evaluation as part of the call process. Tanya thought psychotherapy was certainly a good idea sometimes. Since seminary, she had seen Dr. Wood from time to time.

Tanya did not always listen to Dr. Wood, her psychologist, God, or anybody else. It was a joke among female clergy that they were always keeping a psychologist in business somewhere. Now Tanya was realizing how in the case of Richard she had been somewhere she shouldn't have been.

For the first time ever, when she walked into Dr. Wood's office, she went straight to the couch and stretched out with her arm over her face. She had thought about lying down before on other visits, but she always sat in the armchair. She couldn't truly afford these sessions, since she had no medical coverage these days, but more than ever she needed to talk to somebody where she felt safe being honest. She was ashamed of her behavior, and she was ashamed of her tears. She expected to hear *I told you so*. Of course, Dr. Wood never said what Tanya expected her to say. The doctor was more compassionate and more understanding than Tanya had imagined she would be. Tanya preached grace a lot but tended not to comprehend it for herself.

"He gives you junk. You have every right to expect and demand better than that." Dr. Wood sided with her. "He takes advantage of you. You were vulnerable and lonely."

"I can understand you being attracted to Richard though. He's more exciting than Abdula, isn't he? He is better looking, right?"

Tanya wasn't about to let herself off so easily. She thought. "I'm a fool for getting involved with someone like him…I should know better." She said as much out loud and over and over to herself.

"Instead of beating yourself up for having needs, I think you need to work on what those needs are and how to best fill them, in a way that is healthy and good for you." Dr. Wood set the stage for a new phase of analysis. "You haven't had good examples of loving and caring men. Your husband wasn't that and your father was an alcoholic. You've learned to be quite capable and strong. You are going to have to hone your radar about how to spot a good and caring person who can be emotionally supportive and caring for you. Don't you deserve that? I think you do."

Tanya just didn't feel capable. She felt like she did as a high school student in Algebra class when she simply did not understand the formula, the point, or anything.

"I think you are looking for more than just *nice looking*. That is not going to be as important as "nice". You want a nice man, someone who is going to treat you well." Dr. Wood was right, and Tanya resolved to take her advice. She had to get focused and stop doing things that hurt. There was no question that the church didn't approve of sex outside of marriage, but more importantly, she was being self-destructive and that was hurting her personally. Her professional role was a big part of her self-identity, and it weighed on her so heavily, that she had used her relationships with men and even with Richard to escape from the weight of her own life. He took her out of town, out of her reality, and even sex was an escape from the seriousness of her life. Was it out of character? Yes, it was because with him she could be someone else; she could be different.

****

The professional role was a big part of her self-identity. Four years as a student of ministry at seminary…5 years as the neighborhood pastor of an inner-city church full-time. It was hard to imagine working a secular job. She was used to being in charge. She didn't wait. She was a woman of action and so she was furious with the bishop because he was making her wait and the employers who were making her wait. She went out and bought her telephone because there was no way she would sit around and wait for a man to do something for her. She left the church after all those years because she was tired of waiting for the congregation to sit up and take hold of the mission. She got burnt out because she had done so much of the work herself in the end, even though a lot of it should have been done by church members. She was highly capable, and she was fast. That was a blessing and curse, it seemed. She thrived on having a sense of purpose, a next thing. Now she felt like she was stuck in a room she couldn't get out of, and some days she thought she was going to lose her mind. She was ready to go back to work at some level that she was accustomed to. She had a sense now that what she wanted was in social service. Her job was finding a job. She typed a letter to a program that helped prepare high school students for college, applying for a counselor position. She was going to mail it but decided to drop it off at the county college instead and stop by the hospital to check on the status of her application there.

A few days later she got a letter from the college that informed her that she would not be offered the position, but that her application would be kept on file in case a position meeting her qualifications arose. She called the office and asked if there was a particular reason that she was not even given an interview. Calling the college was probably not a good idea because the director of the program coldly informed her that many applicants were simply more qualified than she was. That remark was a blow she wasn't ready for. Then Tanya found out that the nearest bus stop to the suburban Upper Room Headquarters was about 2 miles away from the site. This information she got from a caseworker at the Chatsworth site, who offered to take her out there on his lunch break. Tanya declined his gracious offer because it was obvious that if a job was that hard for her to get to, it was not going to work out for her. Finally, that afternoon Tanya felt that all she could do was cry herself to sleep. It was time for letting go a little. She rested her resolve and let it flow out onto her pillow as snow began to fall softly outside the window and the twilight fell over her body sprawled out on her king-size bed.

The phone was ringing. She fumbled to get it and got her arm tangled in the covers of her bed.

"Hello." She almost lost her grip on the phone.

"Tanya?" It was her mother's voice on the other end of the phone. She could tell immediately that something was wrong in her mother's world. Tanya could easily decipher her mother's moods by the tone of her voice.

"Hi, Mom. What's wrong?"

"Oh, nothing I just called." Tanya was positive now something was really wrong. Katina Stokes could not hide her anguish.

"I'm glad you called. What's going on?" She sat up throwing her legs over the side of the bed. She glanced at the clock and saw it was 10:15 PM. and she could see it was still snowing.

Katina began to tell her about her cousin who was in the last stages of cancer. She was trying to get a family friend to drive her down to Maryland to see him the next day.

"We were going to go yesterday but Tony couldn't get off from work." Her mother explained.

"I know you want to be there with your brother's son, and I wish I could take you myself, but you know my situation. I would like to be with you."

"I know. I wish it was like it used to be when we could just pick up and go when we got ready." Katina said.

They talked a little while and Tanya told her mom to try to take it easy.

"Don't be getting too upset, Mom. You have to take care of yourself too, you know."

Katina Stokes was 75 years old, but she took on life with a fervor that Tanya hoped she would have when she was 75.

That night Tanya couldn't get to sleep. She had already slept for hours earlier in the evening. She lay awake feeling sorry for herself. She thought about her mom saying she wished it was like it was before when they could just pick up and go when they wanted to. The way it used to be…when Tanya was married to Abdula. They had two cars. They had a beautiful house. The way it used to be…Tanya was a pastor of a church and she had money and membership in a resort club. The way it used to be… they would drive all over the country and take her mom and other family members on trips and retreats with them. The way it used to be…She didn't think she was all that happy then. She divorced her husband because he worked too much, and he cheated on her, and drank too much, and stayed out too much. She left her job because it wasn't stable enough, the dynamism and the economics steadily declined, and she lost some of her own resolve. Maybe she had taken her life for granted. Now all the things she wanted – a house, a car, a man, a job—she realized she had walked away from those things. Now she wanted the things she used to have. She knew her life had never been perfect, even if her mother thought it was, but maybe it *was* better back then.

In her dream, there was a house, a brownstone. She was excited about it, and she went through it discovering rooms. In one of the rooms, it was as if time had stopped in the 1940's. Everything was plush, like the luxurious red upholstered couch, and a red satin robe was laid across an armchair. The walls were papered in a cream brocade pattern with ornate gold trim. She knew a woman had been there, but she was gone now, and everything was just as she had left it.

In another dream, she brought Abdula to the house and she wanted to show him the house and discovered other hidden rooms, through a closet.

In another dream, she discovered a back staircase leading to an apartment. The upstairs apartment was old, worn, and unkempt. It was musty and the green and white floral printed wallpaper was peeling and stained brown. Plaster and wooden beams were exposed through holes in the walls. In the kitchen, there was the petrified corpse of an old woman sitting in a chair.

She had continued through a whole year discovering rooms in her *dream house...* back rooms, walk-in closets that led to rooms behind rooms, and finally a family living there, a family with deep dark secrets. She would see the children and the parents hiding and running in the shadows and behind thick marble columns in long dark halls. These were some of the dreams that filled her nights in the months before she came to a decision that she had to leave Abdula and finally the church. It was an unveiling and a process of discovery, within a fragile framework.

Houses. The tour moved her on through her transitions. She dreamt that she was in an attic and suddenly she became aware that half of the house was falling away. She looked up and she could see the sky through a crack forming in the roof. The whole house was splitting in two. Below her feet, she could see she was on the edge of one half of the floor, as the floor split and she had the sense that she was falling, but she wasn't. The other half of the house just fell away, and she couldn't do anything about it. When she called a repairman, he ran around fixing and she followed him making suggestions about how to make more secure repairs, but he seemed to ignore her.

Her dreams made it impossible for her to ignore her dissatisfaction. They also left her feeling like she had no control. She could pretend during the day. She was good at it, but at night when she wasn't trying, it all came out. Her lack of choice in matters. Life is a cruel trick sometimes. So many things just slip away while we are not even fully conscious. Now she prayed for forgiveness and for strength, as well as for a measure of wisdom. She listened through tears to the lyrics of Yolanda Adams on the stereo: Don't let me make the same mistakes over and over again.

✳✳✳✳✳✳✳✳✳

PART THREE

Mount Up On Wings Like Eagles

One Saturday morning, she woke up to hear the news that a spacecraft had exploded over Texas. She called her daughter who was at college in North Jersey. She wanted to let Mia know that she had put some money in her bank account so she could get any books she needed. Mia was a smart and mature young woman, but Tanya still kept her in the dark about much of what was going on with her because she wanted her focused on school, not worrying about her mother. She also did not want her to think she could help her mother by leaving school. Tanya thought Mia admired her once, and now she wondered sometimes if that would always be true, especially if she found out about all the messes her mother had made in the past year. Mia had kept her grades exceptionally high, and Tanya wanted more than anything to shield her daughter from the fallout of her own personal crises as much as she could. She didn't feel like she was racking up too many points in the motherhood department that morning because she had forgotten about her daughter's birthday earlier in the week.

"I understand you have a lot of things on your mind," Mia said.

Tanya felt like a real jerk. "No, it's not alright. I am soooo… sorry. I don't know whether I am coming or going sometime."

"Mom you gave me money, so I got my birthday present."

"That didn't have anything to do with your birthday…it's just there is so much going on. Forgive me?" Tanya vowed in her mind to surprise Mia and visit her during the week to bring her an actual gift.

Tanya made a sincere effort to be sensitive to Mia's feelings. When Mia was a young girl, she was pretty, although she never quite believed that. She was bigger than her classmates and was often teased. Her cheeks had a rosy tint, her blood right at the surface, a testament to her emotional nature. She was self-conscious and always ready to turn beet red and burst into tears at any minute. She was just as ready to giggle and show a vivacious smile and dancing eyes. When she smiled her whole face, dimples and all, got involved. Tanya always told her that she was, in fact, the prettiest and the smartest girl in her classes and that was the only reason she was teased. Now 5 foot 8 inches, her good looks and her competence were impressive and even intimidating at times. They were both aware of how much they were alike and most of the time that fact bothered neither of them.

As the morning unfolded, news of the shuttle disaster dominated the networks. Seven people dead – Tanya felt for their families, for the nation, and for the world. This public tragedy didn't make her feel any better. She was weepy that morning. She was wounded personally, and this incident just made her feel more like the rug was being pulled out from under her. She decided early in the day to turn off the television and the radio and leave them off. There was no need to listen to tragedy being replayed all day. She had heard enough because she was already on overload.

She was quietly frantic in her mind. She washed the dishes and went to the post office. Then she went to the mall. All the while she let her imagination run wild. She saw a huge bulldozer parked on a street that was being repaired, idle for the weekend. She wondered how much it cost $50,000, $100,000…maybe more. Some people had money, and some did not. She mused on the bus about being on that spacecraft. Some of the people were close to her age she had noticed from the birthdays she had seen on the reports that morning. Born 1957… 1949. Maybe it was her musing about how she could escape from her life because she felt she was headed for something catastrophic. She dreaded going to court and being told to vacate her house, but that was going to happen before the next week was out. She did not have the money to pay her landlord or to move. There was a story on the news the week before about a post office worker who had taken a hostage in a car and a police chase. She had heard about people over the years going *postal*. What if she snapped and went up to the bishop's office and demanded he see her and found a way to make him listen to her story like he cared? If he wouldn't take her seriously then she could refuse to leave his office. What if she staged an outright civil disobedience action on the lawn of his office building? What if she made a spectacle? What if the newspaper's reporters got wind of it? She imagined herself on the news doing a praise dance in front of the bishop's office in protest because he would not find her a call. It was a comical scenario and she thought she must really be losing it to come up with these ideas.

Later she wrote a letter to the bishop on the computer, but she didn't even print it because it was too angry. When she lay down and closed her eyes that night she could not rest easily. A black tangle of cobwebs had taken up residence behind her eyelids and that was what she saw when she shut her eyes. It was frightening, so much so that she couldn't bear to keep her eyes closed. So, she lay there and watched the clock.

After a while, it occurred to her that it might help to read the Bible. She opened it at random and found she was in the Book of Job in the Old Testament. As she read the story she could identify with Job's 'fall from grace'. She could identify with his ignorance of what was going on *behind the curtain*. The story spoke to her, a woman in another time and place – her story of woe and feeling out of control. She knew the feeling of profound loss, the loss of material things, and then the loss of health. Job never lost his place in the scheme of things. She felt she was losing her place.

"Get a grip girl. You cannot lose it. You have to keep it together." She told herself. Then she remembered that if you invite the Holy Spirit it will come. She had experience with that, and it usually worked. Hadn't she preached that to her congregation when her faith was strong? She thought of the ancient chant: *Maranatha…Holy Spirit come.*

"Holy Spirit, come." She prayed in earnest. She felt beaten. No doubt about it she had no strength left and when that happened the only thing left was to turn to God and ask for help. Only God can get a person through.

"Oh God help me. I don't know what to do. I have made a huge mess of everything, and I am counting on you to fix it. I know I don't deserve your help, but I am coming to you because only you can fix this and get my life in order. Please don't let me lose it. I trust you, oh God. Send your spirit to hold me, to comfort me, to keep me. Help me, oh Lord, so that I can rest. I need to rest, but fear is taking over. Watch over me while I sleep. Send your spirit in Jesus' name." She prayed, not knowing if God was listening or not. But she prayed with real need because it was all she knew to do. It was 4 A.M. Peace came.

* * * * * * * * *

It was a short-lived peace only because she was working that Sunday at Lord of Life. She was not preaching, but she was presiding over Holy Communion. She wanted to call her friend and colleague David Black and ask him to get somebody else; to say she was sick, but that would be so flaky. David was the associate pastor at Lord of Life and actually could have done the whole service. He just wanted to work with her, and it was a chance to do a service together because the lead pastor was out of town. She thought it was a great idea when he asked her, but today she felt unable to lead. She didn't know how she could lead two services because she was so exhausted.

When she resigned from her position at New Creation, she started attending Lord of Life because she knew a couple of people who were members there. Besides David Black and his wife, her friend Bonnie, the school principal, and her husband were there. They had been good friends to her, and she had gone to seminary with David. The church was very different from the small African American inner-city church where she had been pastor. Lord of Life was in a suburb of Chatsworth and was a middle-class church with about 500 mostly white members. David, his wife, and a couple of other families were the only black people there before Tanya arrived. Tanya liked the church because it was successful and alive. The people were friendly, and they had a lot of good ministry going on.

The pastor, Rev. John Warren always seemed to preach in a way that spoke to Tanya when she had visited. Maybe it was just that Tanya was listening to the Word in a way that she hadn't been able to when she was the pastor. Whatever the reasons, she was comfortable at Lord of Life. She joined and was not sorry. When she thought she had breast cancer, the members took her back and forth to her clinic appointments, called on her, and prayed for her. She felt very cared for.

That Sunday morning after a sleepless night was the first time she was serving in an official pastoral role at Lord at Life, for they had not pushed that on her right away, recognizing she

68 | JOBETH

was not anxious to be in that role. She was quite comfortable for a season sitting in the back pew worshipping.

After church, she chatted with David outside on the steps of the church. All had gone well, and she expressed her relief about that and how she had not slept much the night before. When she mentioned the eviction she was facing, he told her about an apartment that Lord of Life had that was empty and available.

"I did *not* know that."

"Now you know. I don't think Pastor Warren realizes how bad your situation is."

"Well, I just don't go around telling everybody about all that is going on in my life."

David said. "Well, let me speak to him about it and I will call you tomorrow. That's what the apartment is there for when people visit or in case someone has an emergency."

With that Tanya was given some hope. If she could have that place it would be just what the doctor ordered right about now. She marveled how God always seemed to come through with help even when she could not imagine how she could be helped. Just as she was leaving the building, she realized a man was rushing to catch up with her.

"Pastor Stokes!" The tall thin balding man held an envelope out to her. "I am glad I caught up with you." He handed her the envelope. "I am Steve Caldwell. I am the treasurer. It's my job to make sure you get this."

"Oh… thank you! I wasn't even looking to get paid. After all, I didn't preach."

"Nevertheless, it is in the budget, so here it is."

"And I certainly appreciate it, Steve."

So, she went home that afternoon, deliciously tired. And slept like a baby that night. Even though she had been feeling that she was headed for doom it seemed that God had been looking out for her the whole time.

Monday morning with her arm resting on the top of the open refrigerator door, she wondered about her love affair with leftovers. There were things in containers in her refrigerator that she would never eat and even as cold as it was inside, still it was beginning to smell funny in there. The only reason she was moved to empty out some collard greens that were two weeks old was because she needed the container to put her freshly baked brownies in. So now it became ridiculous not to follow through and get rid of the spaghetti with the fuzzy stuff growing on it and a bunch of other culinary relics.

It was time to move on in other ways too. Just like one needed to admit when a meal was no longer desirable, she needed to move on in her love life too. Richard was *leftover* too long and being with him was no longer desirable. But she had this tendency to just keep holding on to stuff until it started to become rotten and smelly. She had to take responsibility and clean out of her life all of the things she no longer needed. Then she might be available for a new experience. She put some dishwashing liquid into the plastic container, washed it out, drained it on the sink, and then washed the lid. When she was done, she dried the container and put the fresh warm brownies in it. *Now* she had something to look forward to, the refrigerator smelled a lot better and there was room in there to be filled up again. It is a simple thing, cleaning the refrigerator. Somehow doing it gave her a lot of inspiration. The inspiration to do other things she needed to do, like start packing up.

It was time to move out of the house she had been living in. She could easily feel like a victim, who was being attacked by all kinds of evil forces, but, the house was too big, and it cost too much. Her situation had changed. Her call to ministry at New Creation and that neighborhood was over. She had mourned long enough. It was time to move on. But some people need to be dragged out, kicked out, evicted, and convicted in order to move to the next level.

One morning, while Tanya was still packing to move, her doorbell rang. A woman with dark hair was standing at her door. It took her a while to realize it was Candy from the community center.

"Tanya, how are you?"

"I'm fine. Come in. Sorry for the mess. I'm moving!"

"Oh, no. I hope you are not leaving town." Candy said.

"Well, sort of, but really just down the road. How have you been?"

"Oh, I am good. Your background check came back, and I was hoping you could come and work with the program. Are you still interested?" Candy looked hopeful.

"Oh, yes, I am still interested. I'm not moving that far away -- just to Elmsley. When can I start?" Tanya asked.

"Oh, we need you right away. Can you work tomorrow?"

"I will be there! Just tell me where and what time."

Tanya was elated. She loved children. It was only part-time…four days a week, a few hours, but it was better than nothing. She had to ride on the school bus with the 1st, 2nd, and 3rd graders, help teach the reading classes, and help with homework. The children were a delight and gave off a lot of energy. After a few weeks, she felt a lot better.

The new apartment was right on the bus line so she could get to the school easily. She started taking aerobics classes at the church and her spirits and her energy level soared. Because she was feeling a lot better, she accepted some other teaching opportunities that spring. She was glad to volunteer her time to teach a communion class for a few weeks on Wednesday evenings. In addition, she also accepted a paying job teaching adult leaders a Christian Doctrine course once a week on Sunday nights. Life was meager but simpler and she felt she was being useful with plenty to keep her busy. Her friends at the church were very caring and she felt God had brought her to a place where she could heal and grow.

So, she moved into the efficiency apartment on the second story of the church office building in Elmsley. The apartment was located just across the street from the church. She had to part with a lot of furniture and things she just didn't need anymore. The fresh start relieved a lot of the tension and stress she had been living with. She could hardly believe it when Pastor Warren told her that she would not be charged for the space. He felt that the financial issues associated with renting were more trouble than it was worth, and they agreed that theirs was a temporary arrangement that worked out for everybody.

****

"I did you – Pastor Tanya. Your greatest asset is your personality. You are so positive, and you get along so well with people. You have not been at Lord of Life very long and yet you just talk to everybody. You have such an ability to make other people comfortable." Elena, who was the church secretary, was speaking. She was sitting in an armchair very close to where Tanya sat on the edge of the old couch that sank in the middle and swallowed people up. This group of self-proclaimed mid-life women had all joked about how when they sat on that couch, they couldn't get up very easily. She turned to face Elena as she was speaking. Elena had red hair and she was close to fifty years old. Tanya remembered that Elena had interviewed her as a new member about her gifts and interests. Then Tanya felt unable to commit to anything because she had no idea how long she would be at the church.

For the class that day Tanya had asked each woman in the class to say something about the characteristics they saw in another woman in the group. Some of the women said they were quite surprised by the way others described them.

"I did Pastor Tanya too. I just think Tanya is a wonderful person." Barbara said to Tanya, "I knew you before you came here." Tanya sat directly across from Barbara in the circle, and they were the only black women in the group. Barbara was a powerhouse of knowledge and organization despite her quiet demeanor. Somehow Barbara always had a girlish demeanor about her that was the total opposite of the woman she was. She was a corporate attorney by profession, and she was married to David Black, the associate pastor.

Now Barbara was saying to Tanya, "You always seem to truly listen to other people and show compassion and concern for everybody."

Tanya felt slightly embarrassed by the complimentary remarks that Elena and Barbara made. "That's amazing that you see me that way. I have been through some rough times lately, as I have shared with you before. I always think: These people must think I am the most confused, pitiful person they have ever seen!" The women were all saying no and shaking their heads. "I have just tried to keep a positive attitude and to keep believing that everything will work out."

"You really do" Someone agreed.

The sharing moved her. She continued, eager to shift the focus of the discussion. "Well, I did you, Elena. I think you are dependable, and you are always willing to stop what you are doing to help somebody else. You get things done and you are the kind of person I would want on my team."

The other women were nodding in agreement. They were all serious about working on self-development and setting goals in their lives. The exercise that morning was affirming and motivational. It helped Tanya realize that when she resigned from her call, she had been so consumed by anger that she felt utterly defeated. She had been torn down and she had lost touch with the part of herself that was vivacious, fearless, and capable. That morning in the midlife women's class she encountered herself, reflected back at her by this group of women. It was like running into a dear old friend on a lonely road. She was so surprised to run into herself here, in this room, this morning. There she was -- this person so energetic and welcoming, smiling at her as she came in from a long, dusty, tumultuous sojourn. She felt like someone had rushed out to greet her and to announce to her that the hard part of the journey was over. It was as if she heard a summoning to come in out of the cold and enjoy some fruit, rest, and have a soothing drink.

Summer was coming and people were making vacation plans and the church life was flowing into a less hectic mode of activity. The class was ending because of the calendar but Tanya and the other women in the class felt they had begun some new things in themselves. They had made new discoveries on a personal level and had their own plans that had nothing to do with their families and everything to do with their new perspectives, new acceptance, and new resolve. They had things to do with the second half of their lives. Tanya had cautioned them not to allow themselves to lose momentum over the summer but to see how much they could accomplish.

She saw the women as angels who had come into her life to announce that it was the time for which she had been preparing. This was the acceptable time - the time for forgiving and a new beginning, the *kairos* time. She could feel a new tide coming forth. She breathed a deep sigh as she turned off the light and pulled the parlor door closed after the class that day.

* * * * * * * * * *

The tension began to ease in the spring because during the summer when many pastors took their vacations supply preaching opportunities were much more plentiful. Tanya's calendar filled up quickly until virtually every Sunday was booked to preach somewhere in the state. The community center ran a more extensive program in the summer, which included field trips and more recreational activities. It was almost two years since she had resigned from her call at the church. Her life was stabilizing some, where she had felt she was spinning in a whirlpool for some time. She wasn't where she wanted to be, but she felt like she had the basics taken care of. The situation she was in could stay just the way it was for a while, and she would be okay. Tanya wasn't worrying constantly about paying the rent or eating or finding a source of heat or income. She was doing useful work that she enjoyed, and she was preaching. She didn't have to be at the community center until 1:00 pm on Monday - Thursday and she was off on Fridays. She got to sleep in if she wanted to and a lot of times she did. Sometimes she felt guilty because her body seemed to need so much rest. She did a lot of reflecting, journal writing, and praying and she had plenty of time to work on her sermons for Sundays. The best thing about being in a different church every Sunday was that she got to be there and see different practices and people, but she didn't have to feel responsible for anything that was going on in that place. She walked in and walked out, and it was liberating, after being so responsible for so many details of the ministry for so long. It was during that summer that she began to think about what she might do next. She wasn't all that sure anymore that full-time parish ministry was what she truly wanted. Maybe she wanted to be a teacher or maybe she wanted to be a writer. Maybe…go back to school. It had been a long time since she had even considered her true desires. She wanted to travel.

The experience with breast surgery had helped her to get back in touch with some of her oldest and closest friends. As a full-time pastor, she had lost touch with many of her old friends. In the past few years whenever she had a day off or a week of vacation, she felt like a beached whale, barely able to relate to anyone, let alone make the effort to be in touch with old friends. Now she began to make that effort again. Deep down she realized that after the divorce, losing her house, and her resignation she felt she had lost so much, and she was not all that eager to share the sordid details with others. Now as she began to relax and heal, she began to seek support. One thing about getting sick …her friends had let her know in no uncertain terms that they were still there for her, and they missed her. They had vowed to stay in touch, and she tried to make good on those promises that summer.

Although she was on leave from call, she continued to serve on the statewide church council, and in that capacity, she attended the annual statewide assembly. The gathering was held over three days and included a banquet, presentations, and forums on various issues. It was also an opportunity to see people who worked in other areas of the state that she didn't get to see very often. She and Bonnie went to the gathering together and roomed together in the hotel. It was different for Tanya this year because she did not feel the pressure of having to worry about the logistics and organizing of getting her church delegates to the conference. There were definite advantages to not being the pastor of a church.

The national church usually sent a representative to be a keynote speaker at statewide gatherings. This year it was Rev. Linda Olsen, a representative of Global Ministries, a middle-aged woman with platinum-coifed hair, who had a conservative look. Olsen made a few presentations during the assembly and Tanya got to speak with her one evening at a hospitality gathering in the hotel. It seemed appropriate to ask her about global mission opportunities.

"There are certainly many opportunities worldwide. Are you interested in global mission?" The woman responded to her inquiry.

"I have thought about it, occasionally. Right now, I am on leave from call, and I'm open to many possibilities. I'm not sure what God is calling me to just now, and I have been trying to discern where I might be useful." Tanya explained.

"What is your background? Tell me a little about your experience." Linda Olsen looked interested.

"Well, I graduated from the seminary in Philadelphia. I served as a pastor of a congregation in Chatsworth for several years. It was a small African American congregation.

At New Creation, we did a lot of work with poor families and community organizing, as well as the usual teaching and preaching. Right now, I am working with young children out of the public school system in Chatsworth and still teaching and preaching in churches around the state."

"I tell you what, Tanya, we do have openings and we have needs. For instance, some positions need filling in Cameroon and Central Republic in Africa right now. What do you know about that area of the world? Have you been to Africa?"

"I went on a study tour to Africa, to Namibia, and South Africa. What kinds of positions are you talking about?"

"Well, it depends." She seemed to be thinking. After a while she said. "There is an opportunity to work with a women's organization in Cameroon. You will need to learn French. The woman who was in that position for several years has recently resigned. We would certainly like to have that vacancy filled, soon."

Well, that was a new twist. "Oh, well, I don't speak French," Tanya stated, feeling unqualified.

"Oh, we would send you to study the language and then you would go. We'd probably send you to spend a few months in say…Paris."

"Seriously…?" Tanya couldn't believe her ears. This sounded exciting. "The church would pay for that?"

"Certainly! We do this all the time. I think it is worth exploring. Why don't you go onto the website and look at some of the open positions and see if there is anything you would be interested in and then contact my office and you can talk more to someone on our staff."

78 | JOBETH

After her conversation with Linda Olsen, Tanya was psyched. Maybe her prayers were being answered. She had asked God to open up opportunities for her ...but this was much more than she had ever imagined. It was exciting and terrifying. Could she do that? Just leave the country. Go to France...to Africa? Could this be the call-- the inspiring and meaningful call she had been hoping and praying for? She could not wait to talk to Bonnie. They were up late into the night just visioning about what it would be like for her to live in France and to take a call in Africa.

The next day Tanya spoke to the bishop's assistant about it. She found out that if she were to take a call overseas, she would continue to be affiliated with the church in New Jersey. As she discussed the matter, a small voice in her head counseled: ***Don't get too far ahead of yourself.*** Within a week she had penned a letter to Linda Olsen. She had researched global mission opportunities as well as demographics and culture in Cameroon and France. She had set up a meeting with the bishop for mid-June. She was off on eagle's wings with this new possibility.

* * * * * * * * *

PART FOUR

Cry Out Like A Woman

Tanya had a big family. She often wondered what her life would have been like if she had stayed in her hometown. Relatively speaking she was never that far away, but the 100 miles between her in south Jersey and her family in north Jersey was distance enough to live a separate life. That was important to her because she had too many sisters and they had too many children and there were too many comments to be made about everything that went on. Of course, comments were still made, to be sure, but Tanya thought it better not to have to hear all of them or to be concerned about all of them. They were a close-knit family and that had its benefits as well as its drawbacks. They were a family that celebrated birthdays and holidays and special occasions together; a family that gathered around the bedside of their sick and visited each other. Her mother, Katina Stokes, the consummate matriarch, was everybody's mother, and that included the grandchildren and many other community members. Her home was the de facto headquarters for a wide circle of people connected to the Stokes family over the years.

Tanya managed to stay close enough to go home to Newark regularly, for Christmas and other special occasions. Her work as a minister had often required her to work weekends but these days she had less of that kind of responsibility since she was choosing which Sundays she would work, and she enjoyed being able to go and be a little more relaxed and to be able to stay a little longer. She decided it would be nice to go visit her family for the Fourth of July weekend. The Stokes clan was celebrating one of her nephew's 2nd birthday and there was going to be a cookout at her sister's house. It promised to be an enjoyable family time and it was for the most part.

82 | JOBETH

"So, Tanya, when are you going to get another church?" Theresa was asking her. Theresa was 3 years younger than Tanya and she was a nurse by profession. People often said Tanya and Theresa looked alike. But Theresa was shorter, and her skin was a couple of shades lighter. Both of them had put on weight in the last few years and Theresa wore her hair in a short curly style. They were both recently divorced. Theresa, who was involved in a "holiness" church, dressed like a typical "church lady" while Tanya, the main line pastor, tended to sport flat shoes and jeans as much as she could.

"I am not sure I want another church," Tanya responded. "I may want to do something else."

"What do you mean? I think if God called you to proclaim the gospel you can't just ignore that," Theresa said in her matter-of-fact way. "Are you just going to leave the ministry?"

"There is no reason why I can't preach and perform other pastoral functions, even if I am not the bona-fide pastor of a church. I never said I was going to leave the ministry. I just may want to explore other kinds of ministry outside of being a full-time pastor of a church." Tanya said.

"I don't think God meant for you to be in the world. I think you are turning your back on your calling," said Theresa, pushing the issue.

"Theresa, I **am** in the world and so is everybody else, including you. And I never left the ministry. I still preach, teach, and participate in all kinds of ministry. Jesus never separated himself from people who weren't officially connected to religious organizations. Jesus did not separate himself from the world. He intentionally went to people that religious people looked down on," Tanya responded. She was getting heated.

"That's true BUT the Word says that we are not of this world," Theresa countered.

"Oh Theresa, you need to get down off your high horse! Is that what they are teaching over there at your church? People like you are the reason that so many people don't want anything to do with the church. You make people feel like they are not good enough to be in a relationship with God," Tanya said.

"Oh, here we go! Are y'all gonna' start up again?" Erica had just come into the backyard where the family was gathering behind their mom's house. Erica was tall, slender, and regal. She was dark and her complexion was flawless. Her makeup was impeccable, and she was dressed in her usual flamboyant manner with colorful scarves flowing and lots of jewelry. She dressed to impress – always wearing something no one had seen before and that would become the topic of conversation. Erica was the free spirit of the four sisters. She was the most congenial. She was always up for an adventure. Tanya was the oldest of the four sisters and probably emotionally closest to Erica. She got up from her beach chair where she had been sitting while verbally sparring with Theresa and went over to hug and greet Erica.

"Well, the computer whiz is in the house! You know Theresa's got to try to keep me in line. Where did you get that top? You know you ought to give that to me," Tanya said laughing. She was glad that Erica had come to lighten the atmosphere.

Erica spun around modeling her outfit for everybody. "You like this? I've had this for a long time... Hi, Mom." She went over and leaned down to kiss Katina on the cheek, who was feeding Brandon, the 'birthday boy', who sat on her lap.

84 | JOBETH

"Hi, Erica. You know these two," Katina waved her hand as commentary to Erica about the conversation between Tanya and Theresa.

Tanya was so annoyed with Theresa. She thought: *There are Christians and then there are Christians.* She and Theresa were not the same kind of Christians. They were so different that sometimes Tanya wondered whether Theresa was following Jesus or her pastor, or whether the church her sister attended was about worshipping God or were they about worshipping the pastor. Even though Tanya was an ordained pastor for a major denomination, Theresa always seemed to treat her like she was somehow deficient in her understanding of what it meant to be a Christian. Tanya was deficient in her understanding of what it meant to be Theresa's kind of Christian and they often debated every aspect of Christian practice and understanding, very passionately. It was the ongoing "battle of the prophetess and the pastor." The rest of the family dreaded these debates which could go on for hours if they got heated up. Tanya was a liberal Christian who was accepting of people's lifestyles and believed God was gracious enough to willfully redeem sinners. Theresa was a fundamentalist, conservative Christian who judged people based on whether they appeared to be saved according to the standards of her church. Theresa felt called to be a prophet, which seemed to mean, as far as Tanya could tell, that her job was to tell others how to live a proper Christian life. Tanya was an educated ordained pastor with years of experience running an inner-city church and was not about to let Theresa tell her anything.

Regina, Brandon's mother, the youngest of the four sisters, arrived with the birthday cake, shortly after Erica. Regina was the youngest and the most mild-mannered of all the sisters. She had surprised everyone by proving to have a highly technical mind. She worked in New York City as an insurance underwriter. She ran an insurance business with her husband. She probably made more money than all of the other sisters, and compared to her sisters, she remained the sweetheart by nature.

Erica asked. "So where is that handsome husband of yours today?"

"Dan is at the office, unfortunately. Someone has to hold the fort, but hopefully, he will be taking us to the beach tomorrow." Regina held up her crossed fingers as she spoke.

Tanya made a valiant effort to avoid any more debating with Theresa. The sisters didn't get together that often and she preferred to spend this time catching up with them about their work, their children, and their love lives. All of them had been married at least once and they all had children except for Erica. Nobody had pinned her down yet. It was a time for levity, not for the heavy stuff. It was time to cook on the grill and eat. Tanya felt she wanted to just enjoy the moment playing with her young nieces and nephews and reflecting on times gone by. Tanya was aware that if everything went as planned, by this time next summer, she might be thousands of miles away from all of them on the other side of the world.

That night Tanya spent the night at her mother's house and even though Katina was 75 years old she still managed to stay up past ten o'clock talking to Tanya. When Tanya told Katina about the possibility of an overseas mission that she was considering, her mother didn't think it was such a great idea. Tanya didn't know if it would ever happen at all, but she thought she had better let her mom know about it in case she heard it from somewhere else. Katina was involved in the same church denomination and Tanya didn't want her to hear through the grapevine about her daughter leaving the country before she heard it from her. She never expected her mother to accept it easily, because she knew Katina would likely be afraid for her.

Katina had raised her children and stayed put in Newark over the years. In her understanding of life, no one in their right mind wanted to leave his or her family and go running off to another country. Katina stayed with Tanya's father, Charles Stokes, through thick and thin, and bore him six children. Dutifully she cooked his meals every day no matter how drunk he got. He was flawed but he loved his wife and family and Katina always seemed to think she had a good life and a good marriage with him no matter what anyone else thought. Katina nursed him for two years and was holding him in her arms when he died of heart failure at the age of 64.

Tanya thought her mom should have left Charles Stokes, because of his drinking. Dr. Wood told Tanya that even with his flaws she and her sisters and her brother were probably better off with his presence in their life than they would have been without it. That was hard for Tanya to accept because there was pain in the place in her heart where her father lived. He had embarrassed her as a child, and at times scared her, even hurt her physically and verbally. She grew up in a time when, if your father grabbed you by your ankle and held you flailing upside down while he lashed you with his belt, no one called it child abuse. His sagging pants were often smudged with axle grease and food and his knees were always slightly bent. He had three states of mind: drunk, hungover or not well, or remorseful. Tanya was often ashamed of her father, and she remembered not wanting her friends to see her dad. In his drunken rages, he had been known to throw things such as a whole raw chicken or a chair. In Tanya's mind, these were good reasons to leave a man.

Of course, Charles Stokes was not a simple personality. He was a man who was partially blind in one eye. He finally had to have it removed and replaced with a glass one because of glaucoma. Charles was a disabled veteran, and when he received his monthly GI benefit check he took out 'spending money' for himself and handed the rest of his income over to Katina to take care of the house and home. He demonstrated his love for his family that way. Tanya remembered train rides down south to Virginia where his siblings and parents always lived and she did treasure those memories of riding the Amtrak with her father. She also remembered her father taking her and her sisters for long walks while they "window shopped" along the avenue, or down to the waterfront, and once or twice to movies. These things he did to give Katina a break from the children. He could be funny, and he was always around. A neighbor said she would forego the sitcoms on TV to listen to Charles and his friends' antics and banter in the next front yard, under her window, because they were so hilarious. Tanya had a lot of mixed feelings about her dad and her upbringing. In any event, her mom's reality had never afforded her the freedom or the choices that Tanya had in a very different time and place.

* * * * * * * * *

It was a clear day, cool and still. The Chicago sky was bright blue with thin cloudy streaks as Tanya's taxicab pulled up in front of the national church headquarters whose twelve stories shot upward white and concrete. A circular stone structure in front of the building was filled with flowers and shrubbery. It always baffled Tanya how the church could be so corporate, not so unlike the other tall buildings that flanked the courtyard in the complex where it stood. True no shortage of beautiful religious tapestry, sculptures, and paintings were displayed in the huge lobby of the building. A burst of colorful religious expression met her senses as she came through the revolving door of the building.

A lovely and expansive chapel opened off to the right with fluid modernistic carpentry and design, and a church store beckoned on the left, where church enthusiasts could purchase any item they might desire, at any price. Sadly, in Tanya's estimation, the higher the elevator ascended the further one was let down, for beyond the initial abundance of color and grace, the church center was quite sterile. By the time Tanya reached the 10th floor, the headquarters had flattened out to beige and square shapes and straight lines.

A hush fell over fabric-covered partitions that divided huge spaces into personalized cubicles. The artificial plants and flowers, family photos, figurines, and knick-knacks were the only attempts made at individuality in an unimaginative and staid situation where windows did not open because even the air was under strict control. Sounds were muted and the telephones rang softly. The loudest sounds were the occasional elevator bells and the mechanical opening and closing of sliding doors that announced the comings and goings on the floor.

Tanya was seated in a waiting area near the elevators. A polite woman who had greeted her cheerfully disappeared into a maze of cubicles to announce her arrival to interested parties. Tanya noticed that there were some vestiges of the beautiful artwork that was showcased in the lobby, sparingly dispersed throughout the building. Over her head where she sat on a creamy leather sofa, hung a huge, framed photo of

African children with brightly painted faces. On any given floor when the elevator parted, she caught a glimpse of some impressive artifact from another place in the world. It was as if there was a deliberate attempt to inject movement into paralysis: to affect something unchangeable.

"So, this is Global Missions." Tanya thought. She hated to admit it, but she was a little nervous about the interview process that she had been flown into Chicago to begin. Global Mission personnel had arranged for her to come and meet with several people and be back on a plane to New Jersey by nightfall. Waiting was not helping her calm her jitters. Finally, a petite woman with long blond hair and a southern accent came out.

"Tanya? Welcome! I am Margaret Fischer, the Coordinator of African Mission." She was soft-spoken and after the initial handshake, she clasped her hands in front of her and bowed slightly whenever she addressed Tanya.

"We are delighted to have you here. We are so looking forward to talking with you. I apologize for the wait but because of some things that have come up this morning, we've had to change the planned schedule a bit. Jack Anderson, our director had wanted to meet with you first, but unfortunately, he has been called away on an urgent matter."

"Oh, I *do* want to meet him. He has been so very helpful to me over the phone --- answering my questions. I do hope I will get to meet him today."

"In the meantime, are you hungry?"

Food was the very last thing on Tanya's mind. "I had a little snack on the way, but I guess I could eat a little something more."

Fisher was talking. "We thought I could get acquainted with you over lunch as well as tell you a little something about my background and what I do here. I hope to give you some information about some of the options you might consider. By the time we are done eating, our other staff members will be available to have an informal chat with you. Our staff will try to discern, as much as possible, from our conversations today, some ideas about how your interests and strengths would best fit into the mission needs of the global church. It will also be a good opportunity for you to explore any uncertainties or concerns you may have."

Tanya responded with a smile. "Sounds like a plan."

Tanya was a little bothered by what seemed to be a lack of organization. She hadn't expected that. Fisher led the way downstairs to a cafeteria that catered to the church staff and other employees in the adjacent buildings. The food was decent, and Tanya settled on a sandwich, a drink, and a banana. Fisher did a lot of the talking and Tanya learned that she had been involved with Global Mission for eight years and had served as a teacher in South America and parts of Africa. She spoke Spanish and French and had a working knowledge of a few African dialects. Margaret had married a native she met in Somalia three years before and decided that, with their two small children to raise, her family was better served with her settled into a position at the national office, stateside. Her work was closely connected to the wider mission of the church but allowed her to go home and focus on her family at the end of the day.

"I hope that my experience in overseas missions is a resource for people like you, who want to serve in developing nations," Fischer explained.

"I am sure it is helpful. I am sitting here now, trying my best to think of how I can take advantage of your experience – only I hardly know what to ask. I don't want to sound silly." Tanya said.

"There is no such thing. This is your time to find out what you need to know…ask whatever you need to." Fischer assured Tanya.

"Okay. Say you are in Africa, in the Congo somewhere and you need to get home – can you?" Did she sound scared, like she was going to be ready to run home all the time?

"Of course, you are free to do whatever you want, no matter what. On the other hand, you are there to do a job and you will be expected to maintain a certain level of integrity about that. Our staff is committed to your well-being, and we are always ready to support and provide for the needs of any of our missionary personnel. If you need to get home, we will help that happen. In any event, there are furloughs built into your service. You can and will come home, periodically, and you will be expected to visit churches here, in the States, and share your experience with supporters. The church is in the business of mission and a lot of that is about educating and sharing about the church's activity worldwide."

"I spoke to Jack Anderson and Linda Olsen about learning French. Did you have to learn a language? Where did you go? And how hard were language barriers for you?" Tanya asked.

Fischer responded, "I studied Spanish in high school, and I advanced that study throughout my years in college. I also spent some time studying French. There are lots of other people who speak English in most situations where the church is involved worldwide, and people will normally work with you wherever you go. You will be fine in that regard.

92 | JOBETH

We'll give you some information and resources regarding language study this afternoon."

Less than an hour later Tanya found herself in the middle of a half circle of five other staff members. Two were males, both pastors turned bureaucrats. She had met one of the men, Javier Ortega, at conferences a couple of times. The other was a thin balding man who was very energetic and friendly and introduced himself as Donald Sullivan. Margaret Fischer was there and two other women who were administrators. Jack Anderson, Director of African Missions, was not available. Tanya guessed he felt his staff was competent enough to handle her, or maybe he just didn't think she was a serious candidate for global mission.

Tanya focused on the patterns in the Oriental rug, the deep reds and mustard yellows that were woven into an intricate design, and did not pay close attention to all of the background information that her interviewers shared as they introduced themselves. She was trying to still her heart and her nerves and to remember what points she had decided she most needed to make at this interview. In the end, she couldn't remember any of the ideas she had committed to on the plane and decided to just be her best, honest self. This process was about a call, and the Holy Spirit would be leading the way. *Let go Tanya and let God*, she told herself. Besides, it wasn't as if she was so super-clear about the direction she was going in.

Margaret Fischer had said the discussion would be informal and it was that. They asked her about why she wanted to get involved with global missions and what her strengths were. They described a few settings for her to consider and shared several enlightening stories. When they asked about her background, she talked about her upbringing, her trip to

South Africa, and what she had learned on the front lines of urban ministry in the United States.

Ortega asked, "What are your biggest fears?"

"I am concerned about the HIV/AIDS pandemic. I have wondered how bad it is, really, and will I be at risk?" she responded candidly. "I have also wondered about isolation. What is it like? Am I going to be in a hut somewhere out in the jungle? Is it urban? Bustling? Rural…?"

The interviewers seemed to take her concerns seriously as they shared about access to healthcare and precautions that she would need to take.

"AIDS is prevalent in Africa. You need to be careful. What people don't realize is that malaria is still the biggest threat, even more prevalent than HIV/AIDS," Sullivan said with energy. "You will get a lot of healthcare tips before you go, and you will be required to get a slew of immunizations. In Cameroon, there are doctors available and in fact, you'll work very near a hospital.

Fischer added, "There are other Americans in the region, and you'd be working closely with several people and building relationships in the community where you live and work, but cultural loneliness can be very difficult at times. People are affected to a greater or lesser degree and that's why a psychological evaluation is required. It's paramount to determine one's ability to handle that type of situation."

Finally, Tanya spent some time with the two administrators in another section of the building. They gave her the promised information about language study programs, packets with maps, and statistics about the countries they had discussed. They also gave her some information regarding the psychological evaluation and the immunizations she would need to get. By the time Tanya left the headquarters and embarked on her flight back to New Jersey she had pretty much decided that she would be starting a new job and a new life in the new year. With fear and trepidation, she was going forward.

* * * * * * * * *

A month later, Tanya was required to spend a weekend at a nearby college where she underwent an intense psychological evaluation, consisting of of a barrage of tests and hundreds of questions. It was certainly a look within. Having been through several intense experiences in the past couple of years, she didn't feel it was such a bad idea for her to take some time to reflect and make sense of her life. It wasn't costing her anything and Tanya intended to take full advantage of the opportunity. She had been through a similar process before she was ordained. Six years was an interesting interval to check back in on her emotional, spiritual, and mental development.

She stayed at the college in a dorm room for two nights. It was winter break, and the campus was mostly deserted. In between testing and eating, Tanya met with a counselor who talked with her at length about her strengths, experiences, fears, and hopes. The counselor, Dr. Samuelson, wore a yellow blouse underneath her Kelly-green pants suit. She was pleasant with an intense gaze. She was a fair-skinned middle-aged black woman with her dark hair pulled back in a bun on her neck. She evaluated the tests Tanya took and then asked questions based on her assessments. She kept reassuring Tanya that there were no right or wrong answers to the questions she asked.

After a couple of sessions, several issues emerged. Tanya had chosen to stay in a very difficult first call. That was significant and now she was making another difficult, even dangerous, choice for herself by going to Africa. Tanya had been handling isolation and loneliness in her life by having inappropriate and desperate relationships with men. Dr. Samuelson urged her to explore the significance of these choices and to take seriously how extremely dangerous that behavior would be in Africa. She was too comfortable in chaotic and dangerous situations. She needed to seek out healthier experiences for herself which might mean changing her self-perception and her expectations of others. Furthermore, Tanya had to face her anger which seemed to be aggravated by male authority figures in her life, like her father, her ex-husband, and some church hierarchy.

Dr. Samuelson assured her that she had no doubt Tanya was competent and capable of handling the job and that her background would help her cope with especially hard and intense jobs and situations. But she advised Tanya to think deeply about the issues they had discussed and begin to consider solutions.

"Awareness is key. I don't think anything we have discovered is insurmountable, but you have to be honest and make a conscious effort to find solutions and workable healthy ways to proceed. You don't want to be overseas and be in a disastrous personal situation that you can't handle. You need to figure out what you are going to do about these situations beforehand and have plans in place for when the issues arise."

The process was worthwhile. Tanya did not figure out everything, but she committed herself to working on her issues and creating game plans for herself. She wanted to go to Africa, and she certainly didn't want to fall apart over there. She was determined to strengthen herself, develop some self-control, and the ability to handle herself when life became difficult.

* * * * * * * * *

It had been a while since Rochelle and Tanya had gotten together. They had been to college together and both had dreamed of becoming pastors, but Rochelle's life had taken a different path and she had become a nurse instead. Rochelle had decided she wanted to help people, but the politics and traditions surrounding mainline parish ministry in the church had turned her off. The two women had remained steadfast friends and stayed in touch from time to time as they married, raised their children, divorced, and moved around. Rochelle was living in New York, and she was going to be visiting relatives in Philadelphia for the weekend, so they had made plans to get together for lunch. Rochelle was excited about Tanya's plans to go to Africa and there was no way Tanya would leave the country without seeing her first.

Philadelphia was busy as always on a Saturday afternoon. Tanya waited on a park bench in Center City. Rochelle had said that she had a meeting in the area and would meet her at 1:30 Tanya watched an older woman feeding pigeons and enjoyed the sights and sounds of the buses, taxis, and cars navigating the crowded streets as people hurried along. The trees added to Philadelphia's beauty, and she thought what a blessing it was that the founders of the city had written protection for trees into the municipal charter. The city had to work around the trees no matter what and that little fact kept Philadelphia green.

Rochelle arrived at 1:30 as promised. Her bright smile was a welcome sight for Tanya. She was dressed in a brown woolen cape and her shortcut natural hairstyle peeked out from her multi-colored knitted hat, showing some gray around the temples. They embraced and shared heartfelt greetings. They quickly decided to find a place where they could sit for a while, someplace not too crowded or loud. As they walked Tanya asked Rochelle what meeting she had come from.

"It was a twelve-step meeting," Rochelle replied.

Tanya was surprised and hoped she had not embarrassed her friend by asking about something she wasn't ready to talk about. "Oh, I am sorry. I didn't mean to pry…Uh, I just thought it was something having to do with nursing…"

"It's okay. I go to this meeting when I am down here. At home, I am in a program, and I attend several times a week. I will tell you all about it, but first, let's find a place to eat."

When they found a little Asian eatery, they took a table in the back where they could listen to soft soothing sounds of wind and percussion instruments and the high-pitched voice of a woman singing Japanese songs over a speaker. The music did not intrude on their easy conversation. Rochelle was full of questions about Tanya's plans.

"You look great, Tanya. You can just see the light in you! It is so clear! It is so scary, what you are doing, but it seems right. I am coming over to see you. You know I am!" Rochelle squealed.

"You have to!" Tanya agreed. Rochelle had traveled with Tanya as part of the delegation to South Africa. They marveled about how the years had passed since then. They had sung and danced together at several events in South Africa and those memories bonded them together for life.

The native South African students and congregations said that Americans rarely came and entertained them and for that they were grateful. Rochelle and Tanya couldn't help but be excited about the prospect of the two of them in Africa together again.

They ordered spring rolls, shrimp toast, and miso soup, and sipped green tea as they caught up about their families and asked about mutual acquaintances. Eventually, Tanya felt comfortable enough to ask Rochelle about the twelve-step meeting she had attended earlier in the day.

"So, what are you 'twelve-stepping' about?"

Rochelle shared openly with Tanya about the meeting. Tanya was astonished as Rochelle began talking about her relationships with men. Rochelle was given to inappropriate relationships that were based on outrageous fantasy. These relationships had ruined her marriage and threatened her health, safety, and employment over the years. Rochelle had finally realized that she had an unhealthy intrigue with love and sex relationships and that she could manage these relationships better by adhering to twelve steps that changed her life.

Tanya could not believe her ears. She had never known these things about her dear friend. Now she realized that what Rochelle was describing was remarkably like her own experience. She was flabbergasted at the timing of all this because this sounded like a workable solution for her situation. As they talked, Tanya was so relieved to be able to talk about the issue with someone who understood on a personal level and who could offer help. Rochelle confirmed that relief and acceptance were important things that the program offered its participants. Rochelle confessed that she had also recognized Tanya's destructive behaviors but had not wanted to confront her friend unless she knew Tanya was ready to deal with it herself. That day they both decided that their meeting that afternoon was perfectly timed and their long friendship was not accidental. Rochelle invited Tanya to a meeting and gave her a list that included meetings in the South Jersey area. She also advised Tanya to go online to explore international programming. Their struggle was shared by people all over the world. The two women prayed and cried together, both tears of sorrow, as well as tears of joy.

In the next few months, Tanya began to attend the twelve-step meetings and for the first time in her life began to understand and become aware of her tendencies and her ways of coping that involved sex and love fantasies. Tanya took to the program like a fish to water. This was just the medicine she was needing at the time. And it was free. Tanya felt confident that even overseas she would have the tools and support she needed to stay out of trouble. The program would even help with the isolation issue because now she would have access to a support system through which she could connect on a deep and meaningful level wherever she was.

****

In February Tanya had a second interview with Global Missions in Chicago. Her confidence and certainty were evident to Margaret Fischer, Donald Sullivan, and Javier Ortega. Tanya had spent hours poring through the packet of materials she had been given. Besides the conversations with the psychologist during the evaluation and with friends, she also spent hours in prayer and counseling sessions with Pastor Warren. It was clear to her that this was not a matter of practicality or rationality, but it was a spiritual call. As she put her aspirations about Africa into biblical and theological context it was less about assessing safety or gaining financial prosperity than it was about a profound call to be on a journey. She was resigned to trusting God every step of the way, not knowing where all this was leading. She was compelled to be obedient following the biblical examples of Abraham, Jeremiah, the Samaritan woman at the well, and even the young boy Jesus in the temple when he broke away from his family and went to the synagogue to preach to the elders. She was consumed each day with the scripture related to that bible story: "The Spirit of the Lord is upon me for he has anointed me to preach good news to the poor." That became her spiritual.

Tanya shared her strong interest in the women's program in Cameroon. The Global Mission personnel agreed that the Cameroon position seemed like a good fit. The work there was addressing an important need and they had hoped it would be continued effectively. A large piece of that work was about sending young girls to school in a culture that did not hold the education of females in very high regard. A dire need had been identified for scholarships and candidates which required outreach to families to raise their awareness of opportunities for the education of girls and women in their communities. Tanya spoke about the connection between the education of girls and women and other concerns like economic viability and infant mortality rates. By the end of the interview, the team insisted that she meet with Jack Anderson before she left Chicago that day.

When Tanya finally sat across from Anderson, he confirmed for her just how impressed his staff was and how excited they all were about Tanya, and he included himself. Anderson was a large man with a pleasant demeanor and a head of white hair. He sat behind a very clean desk and wore a gray corduroy blazer. Tanya couldn't help thinking either his work didn't involve a lot of paper, or he was a neat freak. Jack gave Tanya contact information for the missionary who had been running the women's organization in Cameroon for close to five years. The woman was an African American woman named Dianna Jordan-Wright who was now back in the United States and was living in Philadelphia. Tanya was anxious to talk with Jordan-Wright because she felt she would be able to fill in the gaps for her.

Talking to Jordan-Wright was important, but more pressing for Tanya was the need to learn another language, and it was a different, harder kind of challenge. It was the next step on a winding staircase to the unknown. She had decided to start with a tutor. That way when she started taking classes she wouldn't be so embarrassed. She hoped to gain a working knowledge of some of the basics before delving into a more formal class structure.

She had decided to go to France for a few months but had been so focused on Africa that she had not thought much about how she would live in France. Fashion, food, and entertainment were not going to be the focus of her Parisian experience and she was faced with the hard fact of foreign language study which had never been her forte'.

A couple of weeks after her second Chicago visit, Tanya was delighted to take the afternoon off from work at the community center to meet Dianna Jordan-Wright in Philadelphia for lunch. They would meet and talk about Dianna's experience at the women's organization in Cameroon and Dianna had suggested that they visit the Francaise Alliance downtown.

102 | JOBETH

Tanya liked Dianna who seemed strong and steady. She wore her head wrapped in a print cloth and a loose-fitting African print garment. Dianna's jewelry boasted the designs and flavor of the motherland. She looked the part and had many stories to tell. Tanya could not help but hang onto her every word. She was pumped and inspired by Dianna.

"It was the most meaningful and rewarding thing I have done in my entire lifetime. It was hard. I am not going to lie, but I wouldn't trade it for the world." Dianna told Tanya.

"What gave you the most joy?" Tanya asked her.

"Living there and learning about the people. Racism is a powerful force in this world. Dark people are suffering in every kind of way – just because they are dark. But they are strong, and I don't see how any of us can go through life not knowing what is going on in Africa. They have a lot to give, and it is in their soul – in their character. I didn't do much, but I was just trying to lift up and stand with some of the women over there. Just trying to see if we could do something together to help them and their children." She just shook her head back and forth. "You are going to love it. You go there to help, but you get so much. I will never be the same."

"So did you help educate girls?"

"Sure. There are a lot of people with money in Europe, France, and the United States – all over. We would raise money; we have access. And we would keep the schools open. Somebody is always trying to close the schools. We did a lot of organizing. And I had to keep stoking the fires – you know, some girl didn't come to school for two days – you have to send somebody – to go get her. Make some kind of deal – find somebody to help at home, you know. We had co-op efforts so that the women could make money, feel accomplished, and support each other. They are fun too. They have a lot of rich culture to share, they are talented in all kinds of ways – I miss them, too. You go- you won't regret it."

"Why did you come back?" Tanya asked.

"It was time. That's all. My family is here – a lot I miss here, too."

Dianna filled her head with colorful stories, warnings, and inspiration and then they made their way down to the Francaise Alliance. Several people had referred to the Alliance when Tanya had inquired about learning French. Apparently, these establishments were to be found in major cities throughout the world and were known not only for the study of the language but also for creating an atmosphere that features all manner of French culture and programs. On that Monday afternoon, she stood alone in front of a bulletin board feeling a little overwhelmed. She wished Dianna had stayed to help her a little longer, but she understood the woman had spent a couple of hours with her and that she did have other things to do. Tanya stared at all the postings, mostly in French, and tried to make sense of some of them. As far as she could tell there was quite a whirlwind of French culture in the area, judging from the multitude of yellow, pink, and blue pastel announcements and bulletins that were push-pinned and thumb-tacked onto the corkboard display. From amongst the clutter, she singled out an announcement about a French tutor with the accompanying curly array of tear-off phone numbers forming a fringe across the bottom of the paper. The announcement read:

FRENCH teacher for hire.

South Jersey area

Will tutor/teach in your home.

Flexible hours – reasonable.

Native speaker – ask for ANDRE`.

Tanya tore a slip of paper with the phone number on it from the bottom of the flier. That evening she called, and two minutes into the conversation she was sold, because of the accent, of course. Andre could have been selling pipe cleaners and she would have wanted to meet him.

Andre Benoit was charming and a good teacher. He took his time with Tanya and did not make a big deal about her lack of knowledge. He applauded her commitment and her desire. He encouraged her a great deal. His rates were manageable, and they began right away meeting 3 times a week for an hour each time. Andre was about 6 feet tall and had a well-developed build. His skin was caramel tan, a blending of his French and African heritage. His mother had made sure he learned her native French even while he grew up in the marshlands of Louisiana, where his father's people had deep roots. His family had done well in real estate and interior design and that afforded his mother many travel opportunities which was her heart's desire. She never tired of flying to Paris and spending seasons in the south of France and she liked the idea of having her son study abroad as much as possible.

Andre told Tanya, "My parents spent so much time apart they came to like it that way. After they parted ways for good, I had to decide what I was going to do with my own life. I grew tired of traveling to and fro...real estate is stressful, and decorating did not interest me at all. I finally settled on teaching as a suitable profession, so I decided to come to the East Coast and get my teaching credentials. So here I am."

He bowed in an exaggerated manner extending his hand as he did. "I am at your service."

"Lucky me…not so good for you," Tanya said half-jokingly.

"You are no different from many of the students I have taught. I have been helping people learn the foundations of the French language for 5 years now. So, shall we get started?"

"Let's do it!" What Tanya lacked in knowledge, she made up for in determination and enthusiasm. Her brain was resistant to accepting new ways of saying the simplest things. She had to admit that, as so many people had warned her, learning the language at her age was no easy endeavor. She studied hard and listened to tapes and mumbled under her breath at work and on buses and in restaurants a lot as she conjugated and memorized. She was making slow and painstaking progress. When she was with Andre, she greeted him in French and used French expressions in conversation with him as much as she could.

* * * * * * * * *

PART FIVE

Holy Song In A Strange Land

Tanya felt stressed. She was either working, in class, studying, or at a meeting and she was feeling like her life was all drudgery. She was attending church but had little time to socialize. One day, feeling she needed to break out of her routine, she decided to cook dinner with several courses, even though she was scheduled to study with Andre that evening. She planned to surprise him by arranging for them to take a break from studying and she had even rented a French movie with subtitles. By the time it was all done she had low light and candles going. Andre was very surprised when he arrived. Tanya greeted him at the door in a form-fitting knitted sweater that had a plunging neckline that she had paired with a short denim skirt and some black boots that she thought made the most of her long legs.

"Tanya this is all very lovely…but you don't have a lot of time to prepare yourself. I am not sure this is the best use of our time together." Andre said.

"Oh, it is only one evening, Andre. We have been so diligent, and I just wanted to show you how much I appreciate what you are doing. It's time we took a break. Now sit down. Just relax." She whined and pretended to pout. With that and without thinking she kissed him lightly on his cheek and then hurried off to get wine.

"Red or white?" She asked as she opened the refrigerator.

Andre just threw up his hands and sat down at her glass-top table set with flowers and candles. He shook his head and said, "Tanya you are remarkable. I see you have gone through a great deal of trouble."

"It was not so much trouble. I wanted to do it. What trouble? A handsome man, *bona petite*! Enjoy!" She walked over to the table and poured the wine into their glasses.

108 | JOBETH

"Tanya you will begin your class at the Alliance soon. We must prepare." He sounded concerned. "I appreciate this tonight; however, I have your best interest in mind. I want you to have every advantage."

"I am going to be fine. Now the feast…I hope you like chicken." She was setting the steaming platter with the carefully prepared poultry garnished with greens on the table. She followed up quickly with a bowl of roasted vegetables.

"Ah, *magnifique*." He put his fingers to his lips in the gesture of a kiss. "Now tell me of your plans. When will you go to Paris? Have you been before?"

"This summer I will go. And no, I have never been." Sitting across from him, Tanya was mesmerized by his intensity.

"Then I must tell you where to go. There is much you should see. Paris is a wonderful city. I will tell you everything."

Tanya was fascinated with his sharp good looks and his curly hair shining like black coal in the candlelight. A loose lock of it fell over his left temple whenever he bowed to take a forkful of food. She knew he was only thirty years old, but she was quite impressed with him as a teacher and as a person. His eyes moved in the light, enormous and dark. She liked it when he allowed himself to gaze into her eyes. She felt drawn into him. He had a way of giving her such intense focus that she began to be convinced that he was as attracted to her as she was to him.

They ate the dinner and some cheesy crepes drizzled with a delicious sauce for dessert. She was all set to start the movie and invited him over to the loveseat while he made a point to compliment her profusely about the meal. It was the first time they had sat anywhere other than the dining room table in her small quarters. As she became more intoxicated with the wine which she refilled a third time, she leaned over him to reach for the film and to refill his wine glass and she wondered if he liked the perfume she was wearing. She was aware that her skirt was short and that when she sat down or bent over her ample thighs were half exposed. A couple of times she caught him looking at her legs and she was pleased about that. Andre stayed for a bit of the movie and then apologized that he would not be able to see it through because of an early class the next morning. Tanya was disappointed that he suddenly had to leave. In the end, her fantastical evening seemed to end prematurely.

* * * * * * * * *

The next day Tanya had to face the reality of the previous evening, without the haze of alcohol, and she was ashamed. She finally called Elva, who was her sponsor in the sex/love addiction program she had become a part of. She felt bad and she feared she had ruined her relationship with Andre, as much as she needed him. Andre had called early in the day to tell her he wasn't coming back to continue their French lessons. He assured her it was because lately he was getting more work in Philadelphia, and it just wasn't very convenient for him to keep up instruction with her in New Jersey. He gave her some names of other tutors in the area. She couldn't blame him. Sure, a younger man could be interested in an older woman, but she had no reason to believe that Andre was having these kinds of feelings for her. The fact was that she had come on to him and she had made him uncomfortable! She realized she had been inappropriate and destroyed their relationship – a professional relationship that she needed.

Abuse and destruction had a way of marring her intimate relationships because Tanya was molested as a child. She preferred to forget all of that ugliness and hide from the fact of her confusion that began at a very young age at the knees of one of her elementary school teachers. There was a time when she used to think about it all the time and was frequently reduced to tears about it. Now it seemed exposed again, after Dr. Samuelson's counsel. Time had passed and she had just about buried it in a place inside herself where it could not have such an overt control of her emotions. When an adult breaks the trust of a child it is a dark day, and that cloud can blot out a lot of light. Now that she was dealing with her obsessions around sex and love she was learning that her past still had power in her life. Her past had an insidious influence because Tanya allowed it to lurk unchecked. That little girl who was manipulated into a sexually intimate relationship at a young age was still trembling afraid and ashamed when it came to intimate relationships. She had done something wrong; it was her fault and she just needed to get it right.

"I am always trying to find love, but I guess I don't truly know what it is. I am like a whore. I hate to admit that. I am. But then whores are not supposed to be crying because a 'john' doesn't turn out to be Prince Charming or a knight in shining armor. I am pitiful!" Tanya was saying into the phone.

"You are not!" Elva said, "You don't need to be turning over every rock looking for love. Love doesn't hide from you, so you have to go and find it. Love is all around you."

"I know that...sometimes – I think. But I get so lonely. I get scared. I get desperate and I think I will always be alone, and love won't find me."

Elva asked, "Why? Why do you think you aren't loveable? You are great. You are smart and good. You help so many people. You are fucking fantastic. Look at the things you have done, what you are doing. You ARE love!"

"Well, thank you, Elva." Tanya's eyes had filled with water while Elva was talking and now a tear spilled out and she swiped at her cheek with her free hand. You make me feel so good when you say that. I just have to try to remember that love is not sex at the moment when I need to remember it. And that sex is not even the best thing I have to give…I treated *him* like a whore. I was paying him to be here, but he didn't have to put up with that!"

"So, what do you do?" Elva challenged her, and then said with conviction, "You recognize! You make amends where you can. This may or may not be the time for that. At least you are not in denial – you see the error of your ways. Watch yourself. What was going on with you? I haven't heard from you much lately. How is your daughter?"

"I see your point." Tanya had to keep in mind that the scared little girl inside of her always wanted to get her off into a corner alone like her molester pushed her into the cloakroom after the class was empty. Alone the evil could overtake Tanya and destroy her. She did need to be more conscious of the hurtful forces present around her.

* * * * * * * * *

Richard called. He apologized to Tanya for not being there for her the way he should have been.

"Forgive me, baby. I miss you. I need to see you." Richard was direct. "Let me take you out. I will take you to that place you like up on Route 1."

"Richard, I don't want to argue with you. I can't take you right now. I don't have time for your nonsense."

"That's great, baby. I promise I don't want to fight. I just want to hear all about what you are doing. You're always doing something. That's what I love about you." Richard said. "How is Mia?"

"She is doing great. It just so happens I am planning a birthday celebration for her this weekend."

"Nice," Richard said. "Are you going to invite me?"

"Richard. I don't have a problem with inviting you to anything, but you cannot take over the situation and start arguments with people about stupid stuff." Tanya felt herself folding, even as she put up protests. The truth was she missed him too. Somehow it still felt like he was a part of her.

"I promise I won't do anything like that. Hey, are you still going to Africa?"

"Yes, I am. But it's very complicated. I have a lot to do in preparation before that happens. I am learning French right now." She kept quiet about the fact that she had run off her French teacher.

"That is why I have to stay focused, and I can't be getting caught up in a lot of drama."

"Baby, I am so proud of you. And you sound great. I can't wait to see you." He sounded genuine.

Tanya hung up the phone, shaking her head. She believed him. There was a connection between them that she could not deny. There was also a lot she did not understand about their relationship. It left a lot to be desired. The fact was that they were both struggling with complex issues and sometimes it was a volatile mix. Tanya recognized that Richard's family business was virtually dead, and he was not trained to do anything else. He was a person who had been born into a comfortable lifestyle, given everything he wanted and when circumstances changed, he was left without solid footing and was having a hard time finding stability of his own. He was struggling late in life to find a path that made sense and he just wasn't very well equipped. On the one hand, she knew he needed her and on the other hand, she didn't want to take all that on. He wasn't accustomed to being gracious, appreciative, or humble. His method of operation was to hold all the cards and have everyone look up to him. Her attraction to him had nothing to do with his position or his family's position; she wasn't from around there anyway. She fell in love with him for him and he related to her in a way that he couldn't relate with many others. He gave her the opportunity to step outside of a role, and similarly, she afforded the same for him.

Tanya was excited about the party she was planning for Mia. She felt she had neglected her daughter, so she called her at school and proposed that she make some of her favorite dishes and invite some friends, her grandmother, and her aunts for a birthday gathering in her honor.

"That would be nice." Mia liked the idea of being the center of her mother's attention for a change.

"Why don't you make a list, and I will send out some invitations. Or if you want, I will make up some invites and you can give them out."

"That would be better, Mom. I will give them out to my friends and reach out to people and you can take care of the family and whoever you want to invite." Mia said. "Thanks, Mom! I can't remember the last time I had a birthday party!"

"Yes, this will be fun." Tanya was enjoying the planning. She was cooking three main dishes: a curried chicken, Chicken Creole, and a barbecue chicken and she would have ice cream and cake. She had arranged to hold the gathering in the recreation room at the Lord of Life Church Hall because her space was entirely too small for the event. Her sisters and her mom were coming down early that Saturday to help with the decorations and set up.

Elva commended her. "This is a much healthier activity than trying to seduce the French teacher. You must spend time with your loved ones. I am proud of you, and these are the things that will strengthen you when you are away next year. Only be careful with the lover boy, Tanya. Don't let Richard rain on your parade."

"Oh, I am not going to let that happen. I have already warned him." Tanya said.

"And I am warning you." Elva retorted.

The party planning was in full swing. Tanya felt good about having a festival and making a genuine attempt at socializing. Even inviting Richard felt good in some ways. They had not often been on the social scene as a couple. Too often she kept her personal life under wraps because of her position as an unmarried female pastor in the community. Maybe it didn't have to be that way. Maybe this party would be good for her and Richard.

* * * * * * * * *

The Stokes sisters, Erica, Theresa, Regina, and their mother Katina were at the door early on Saturday morning, as planned, bearing gifts, food, and decorations. They were anxious to get over to the recreation hall to get everything set up. Katina was pleased with the whole idea of the party. She was certainly progressive and proud of her daughter's accomplishments and independence, but caring for family – this nurturing role, in her mind, was the crowning glory of a woman. When she saw Tanya in this light, she couldn't be more proud, and besides her grandchildren were her joy. Much to Tanya's vexation, Katina was also obviously glad that Tanya had a suitor attending the party, Richard, who Katina found somewhat charming. He did have a knack for impressing elderly women, using flattery, and being especially attentive to them.

Tanya donned a flowing, floor-length, orange, and blue sheath with a swirling print for the evening. She twisted her dreadlocks into an up-do and fastened them with a long, jeweled clip to hold them high up on her head. She wore some dangly earrings and comfortable shiny flats. She didn't bother with much makeup, just lipstick, because if it got hot, it would be senseless. The colors of her outfit were glowing enough without enhancement.

As the guests began to gather, Mia was overjoyed with all the attention she was getting. The aunts fawned over her with gifts and cards. It was unusual for her to have her family and her friends from college together for the event. Some of her friends even brought flowers and gifts of cookies and candy for her mother. Tanya was impressed with their consideration and their respectful gestures. While she stood near the door watching Mia socialize with the guests, she couldn't help thinking that her daughter was close to perfect and that she truly was something to celebrate.

The church hall was a long white room dotted with round tables. With the decorations, one could almost forget the regulation basketball fixtures mounted at both ends of the room. The décor was basic enough so it could be dressed up to suit the occasion as needed. For this event, everything was draped in shades of electric blue and sky blue, replete with crepe paper streamers from corner to corner across the room, and silver stars hung from the ceiling. Erica, the aunt with the largest penchant for flair had supplied the appropriate decorations. Of course, they would never have been hung so artfully, were it not for Regina's diligence in seeing the process through all afternoon. Tanya and Erica had run back and forth to the store and fussed over getting the music set up all day. Tanya had done all the cooking she intended to do the night before. It was Katina, the dutiful matriarch, who was the only one willing to listen to Theresa's religious platitudes, ad nauseam. Those two were left to the kitchen details of setting out the food and preparing the last-minute salads and *hors d'oeuvres*. Theresa told their mom of prophecies and recounted her pastor's sermons while they worked. All the time Katina had the good sense to nod her head, ask the occasional question, and make all the appropriate sounds which was all Theresa needed to keep her going.

When the party got underway at about 7:00 in the evening, people seemed to be enjoying themselves as they greeted one another and gave warm birthday wishes to Mia. Soulful R&B tunes helped create a party mood. The food was set up buffet style on a table with an elaborate birthday cake as a centerpiece. All the Stokes women were feeling pleased that they had put together quite a posh event.

At about 8:00, Richard arrived. He was dressed neatly in a black sports jacket and khaki pants. He had on a cream-colored shirt that was open at the collar and brown shoes. He greeted Tanya, who was still standing close to the door when he arrived, with a light kiss on the cheek. He cupped her chin in his hand and said, "My dear, you look like the *rose of Sharon.*"

Then in his gregarious fashion, Richard entered the room and all heads turned as he greeted Katina Stokes. "Mom, as always, you look like the queen of the ball that you are…and it is no secret where your daughters get it from."

"Oh Richard, if you say so…" Katina was smiling and blushing as she hugged him.

Richard made the rounds, to all the sisters. He reared back with his arms outstretched and made comments to all the sisters that made everyone anxious to hear what he would say next. Finally, as he approached Mia, he produced a medium-sized white box with a red bow tied to it.

"Mia! Happy Birthday, Mia. You know I had to get you something." He gave her the box and she was obviously, as surprised as Tanya was. One just never knew what Richard was going to do. Sometimes he could be so impressive, Tanya thought, as she watched Mia open the gift, a small delicate jewelry box that made music when you opened it.

By this time, it seemed that most of the guests had arrived. Tanya turned the music down low. "I just want to welcome everyone and thank you all for coming. We'll get to sing Happy Birthday to Mia a little later. In the meantime, let us give thanks, because every time, I look at my daughter, Mia, I know I am blessed, and we should give thanks for the blessings we have. It is important to show gratitude."

Tanya clasped her hands and bowed her head. "Thank you to God, our creator and our provider for allowing us to celebrate another blessed year, for Mia, and for this food. Thank you for my mother, Mia's grandmother, and my sisters, and their loving and helping hands. Amen?"

"Amen!" The collective response was lifted in the room.

Tanya raised her head and threw up her hands. "Please help yourself to the food and enjoy the music and celebration!"

With the music back on it was louder and more rhythmic than before. A few couples took to dancing in the large space that was clear in the center of the room. Other people moved to the buffet table to get plates of food. Tanya went into the kitchen to see if she could get Katina to abandon her apron and sit down for a while. Katina agreed that everything seemed to be under control. Tanya was able to get her mom out of the kitchen and seated at a table. Richard came over to sit with them. Dancers were moving on the floor. Richard asked Tanya to dance to "Smooth Operator" and after that, he took Katina for a brief spin, too. Just then Elva walked in, moving quickly. She was looking around for Tanya and when she spotted her, she hurried over. She greeted Katina and Richard briefly but grabbed Tanya's arm to pull her away from the table. Elva lowered her voice "I think you have an unexpected guest." And looked in the direction of the double doors that opened to the hall. Framed in the doorway stood a figure that made Tanya's knees weaken A gasp stuck in her throat as her heart skipped a beat. She was not the only one who was noticing. Heads were turning in his direction, because Andre's chiseled features, flawless smooth skin, and shiny curls were not to be ignored.

Elva explained. "He was around the front ringing your bell. I knew who he was before he even told me." As Tanya started walking toward Andre, Elva whispered, "Damn, girl! I can see why you were having a hard time with him."

120 | JOBETH

Tanya managed a welcoming smile, holding out her hand to Andre. When he smiled back, it was as if light filled the whole room. Andre bowed with one arm behind his back, as he took her hand and gently kissed the back of it. As he lowered his head, she saw his eyes close and felt like Cinderella. She knew how silly that was. He stood up straight and looked down at her, and still holding her hand, placed his other hand on top of hers. He cocked his head to one side and spoke. "Please forgive me for coming unannounced. I was passing by, and I stood in front to call you. Your friend, Eva? She assured me ..."

"Elva...my friend...but no, it's fine. Come in. You are welcome!" she said, gesturing toward the room full of people. "My daughter's birthday...a celebration. Please stay. Have something to eat. Let me get you something to drink."

"I see. How wonderful," he said. "I *will* stay a while. You don't mind?"

"No, not at all! Please make yourself comfortable." She went to get him a soft drink.

Of course, her sisters and Mia wanted to know who he was. While she was at the table getting him a drink and some snacks, she had some explaining to do. She could not avoid Richard's curious looks either. Katina was pretending not to notice anything.

"Just stop it! You all...he is a friend, actually my French tutor...okay?"

"Well, okay," Theresa said. "But are you sure that's all there is to that?"

Tanya didn't bother to answer her, as she carried the plate of food and the drink over to where Andre was now seated at one of the round tables. A couple of Mia's friends were sitting there too, and Andre was chatting with one of the guys. He rose to stand when Tanya approached the table. She sat the food down in front of him.

"Thank you, Tanya," he said almost whispering in her ear. "By the way, you smell fantastic."

She sat down with Andre while he ate. When Mia was nearby, she motioned her over so she could meet Andre.

"Andre, I'd like you to meet my daughter, Mia, our guest of honor tonight. Mia, this is Andre Benoit, my French Tutor." Tanya said.

The two exchanged pleasantries and Andre wished Mia a happy birthday. When Mia left to join her friends, Tanya turned to Andre to get some answers.

"I have to say I was surprised you came. I didn't think I would see you again."

"I know, but I thought about it, and I decided…you need me. I believe I know what you need to do and your time frame. I know I can help you learn more. This is why I should come back." He was smiling brightly.

She laughed. "You are right, Andre." She sobered. "I apologize for treating you the way that I did. It was wrong and I won't do it again. I do need you and you are a wonderful person to realize that…to even care, you are a wonderful person…" She sputtered, her voice beginning to crack. "Andre, do you forgive me?"

"Yes. I do. I admire you for what you are doing." He paused. "You are a beautiful woman. And the more I think about it, and I have thought about it plenty…" He smirked playfully.

"Look. Don't feed into my illusions, Andre. Don't do it. You were right! Learning French is where I need to focus right now." Tanya interrupted him. "I have appreciated your friendship, your concern, and your help. That is enough. The truth is I don't need to be involved in any romantic relationship right now. I have a lot of things to work through and this mission overseas is my priority."

Just then she saw Richard hurrying across the room, headed for the exit. He looked at her but kept walking. It had been at least forty-five minutes since his presence had even crossed her mind. She watched him push the doors open and leave. She was thinking she should go after him and say goodbye, but she did not. She turned her gaze away from the door closing behind Richard. Andre was using his napkin as he finished his food. Suddenly he looked so very young. "Let's talk on Monday and set up some study dates," she said.

****

Just as the door closed behind Richard when he left Mia's birthday party, another door opened for Tanya somewhere in the depths of her being. The light from that opening warmed the dark spots in her mind. She stopped floundering in the shallow, mucky water where she was wading. She began to see the possibilities of her future coming into hazy focus in the distance. Now that she could sense her path, she could mobilize her determination and strike out on it. She saw Andre for who he was, and he could be a lot of things to someone like Tanya. Going to her 12-step group and her hard work with Elva helped her to see how her behavior was diseased. She called it *fantasia*, an itchy condition that caused her to manufacture dreams and flighty scenarios. Her fantasia could take her to a lot of places, and some of those places were good and useful, but it was also the vehicle to some most regrettable ditches. She was learning to be careful, to pay closer attention to where she let herself get to. Andre was not her lover! Richard was not her supporter! The next couple of months she worked harder than ever studying French, using the CDs for practice and reviewing her notes during whatever free time she could find. She could see there was no way to get around the tricky storms and sea monsters that haunted the deep trenches between her and her destination.

Her fears were a challenge and managing them was the hardest work she had to do. She got intentional about setting up defenses for herself like weekly lunches with Dianna, where she learned more about the women's program in Cameroon and discussed African culture and history in the area. Another week, she gained strength from going to a couple of extra support group meetings. She stocked up on motivational books and movies with French subtitles. She tackled her classes at the French Alliance with diligence and had coffee with people who had traveled to France in the recent past.

As she flipped the days on the calendar, she guarded against her anxiety taking over. She was grateful that she hadn't lost Andre as her tutor. Now when she saw him, she didn't waste time thinking about romantic trysts, but milked him for knowledge, hanging on his every word. He was very pleased with the rapid pace of her learning. At the end of their last study session, he said as much.

Your hard work is paying off!" Andre looked earnest as he spoke. He continued. "I think that you have prepared yourself well and you should do very well in your class. You should be proud."

"I don't know about all that! But I couldn't have done anything without you. Thank YOU. Especially thank you for not quitting on me." She bowed her head, slightly averting her eyes.

"Tanya you need not regret anything." He waved his hand in impatience. "Go now. Do what you have set out to do. I think that you have a great new adventure in front of you. I think what you are doing is fantastic and brave. A lot of people are not so brave." He was smiling broadly. "When are you leaving for Paris?"

"Next week. My classes start there two days after I get there." Little snatches of wind were catching in her throat as she was speaking. She felt giddy and chuckled. "Andre! I can't believe I am doing this. I even forgot this was our last session! I have a check for you, but I should have done something else... a gift...something special..."

"No need! Not at all." He protested. He pointed his finger at her. "Stay in touch. I want to know how you are doing. You will stay in touch?"

"I will. I will." She promised.

"Now... I brought YOU something." He held out an envelope. "Here is a list of places and things you should see in Paris. I have included directions and some people to contact. Some of these people are personal friends. They will be glad to help you, so don't hesitate to call."

The next couple of days were consumed in a whirlwind of shopping and packing. By the time Mia dropped her off at the airport, Tanya was exhausted. Spiritually she had gone to the place where she felt totally helpless and totally faithful. All she had was her faith and this was what she was clinging to. No friends, no family, no guide, and no point of reference. The tug of the call was the only thing leading her now. She repeated and hummed an old song under her breath as she checked her bags and made her way through the airport: *I don't believe He brought me this far to leave me. I don't believe…No, I don't believe…I don't believe He brought me this far…to leave me.* On the plane, as it taxied into position for take-off, with the seat locked into an upright position, she was lifted up and away.

* * * * * * * * * *

Dear Mom:

All I have ever heard is how the French people are snobbish and rude. It seems Americans always criticize the French. I have decided that Americans have their issues, and my strategy is to kill the French with kindness… It is working for me, so far. I bring them flowers. I leave them nice little notes. I am polite to shopkeepers and I find that my neighbors look out for me and that the merchants and shopkeepers look forward to my coming. It is not so bad. Paris is a beautiful city, though I regret I don't have more time or money to spend on it.

How are my sisters? Tell them to start saving their pennies because I was thinking we should all come over here together for a real vacation. Tell Theresa that she would love the old churches that are so beautiful, and I know Erica would love the shopping and fashion. Miss you all. Love, Tanya

Dear Elva:

How are you, friend? How I miss you! I am flying by the seat of my pants…you and I both know this is not good. I can imagine myself "acting out" in a minute with some sexy Parisian gigolo! Luckily, and thanks to you, I did contact Jean and she is helping me to stay on the straight and narrow. I AM on my best behavior. Jean is delightful! She came and picked me up and we went to a gathering of very beautiful and spiritual people. They talked about how easy it is to get "intoxicated"

126 | JOBETH

here. This is, by nature, a city of intrigue! They warned me of the common pitfalls. Some people here, apparently make their living off exploiting the Parisian fantasy. I feel safer just having the connection with the fellowship.

I am studying very hard! I don't have much time to socialize. The biggest danger is all the time I spend alone, especially the evening hours... gratefully, I study so hard all day that I am exhausted most nights after eating. Love, Tanya

Dear Andre:

Thank God for you! I loved the Moulin Rouge. I have taken some time to ride the subway and visit some museums. Thank you for putting me in touch with your friends, too. They have been very accommodating and have steered me to the best eateries and markets. Daniel made me promise to give you, his greetings. He seems to think very highly of you. With Daniel and Marguerite looking after me I don't have to feel I am being taken advantage of out of ignorance! I miss you so much and not a day goes by that I don't wish I could ask you some questions, but all and all, my studies are going well. I have often surprised my instructors. I have been learning from the best. I know I will never be able to truly repay you. Not ever. Merci. Best, Tanya

Dear Rochelle:

How is it going? Hope you and your family are well. Paris is a dream. Surreal seeing the actual images you have only ever seen on postcards and in books! It is more beautiful than I can describe in words. You have to join us when the sisters do their stint abroad. In the meantime, I hope you have started planning in earnest for your trip to visit me in Africa. We will have to find a church that will let us dance in praise *of our Lord like we did in Namibia! I can't wait. What about you? Write soon.*

Love, Tanya

Dear Mia:

I miss you so much. I hope

are doing well and that you are doing well in school. Now that I am here, I wish that you had taken off the semester and come with me. I am starting to believe that the education we get from life experience trumps what we can learn in the classroom or just from reading. I think we could have had the time of our lives over here together. Of course, I would have failed my French courses hanging out with you. ;-) Oh well, it is a hard choice, but that is what I think because I am so far away from you.

Love, Mom

* * * * * * * * *

In the fall, Tanya returned to the States from France just long enough to say her last goodbyes and to ship ahead some of the things she imagined she would need. Dianna had warned her not to bring too much stuff with her to Africa because it would only make her feel ridiculous. She explained to Tanya, "In the less developed world people get along with a lot less stuff. You will be surprised."

Tanya was glad to have one last lunch with Dianna before she left for Africa. even though Tanya was wound up with her own anxiety, she noticed that Dianna was pensive over her tea. Tanya was feeling exhausted from packing and was worrying about forgetting something.

Dianna said. "So, when is the last time you spoke to anybody at Global Missions?"

"It's been a couple of weeks. I thought someone would call me again, but they haven't. I was debating whether I should call them, but I probably shouldn't expect them to hold my hand through everything."

"They won't." Dianna was quiet for a moment. "I got a call from Geyali...she says they are hearing noise from the militia groups in the north. She said more people are coming into Cameroon every day...it seems the wars are getting worse. I can't believe Global Mission hasn't said anything to you."

"Who is Geyali? So what? Should I call...?"

"Geyali works at the mission offices in Yaoundé and Doula. She is native but has been trained as a mission worker by World Hunger Federation which is an interdenominational church organization. She is the Senior Director of the Women's Center where you will be working. We have managed to stay in touch since I have been back. Maybe it isn't as bad as it seems." Dianna sounded hesitant. "Chicago usually keeps abreast of these things..."

"Well, now you are making me uneasy! But I would think that if Chicago hasn't alerted me then everything is a *go,* and I shouldn't worry."

Dianna pulled out a small notepad and scribbled on it. "Here are some websites. You should check in with these sites regularly because they run frequently updated bulletins about what is going on in various regions, just type in Cameroon and other related areas like Chad or Nigeria and they will state what the activity is. You are going to have to stay informed now."

Tanya was on alert from that point forward. She was somewhat annoyed with Chicago officials for leaving her in the dark. Later that day she did put a call into Jack Anderson, the Director of Global Mission, and Margaret Fischer, the Coordinator of African Missions. Neither of them answered, but she left messages asking them to call her back. She made of point of mentioning that she was slated to be on a flight to Cameroon within the week.

The next morning, she still had not heard anything from Chicago. She called Fischer again and spoke to her administrative assistant. When she expressed her concerns about rumored violence in the area where she was headed, the woman assured her that if any of the missionaries were in danger they would be informed and that she should feel confident that the organization would never put their personnel in danger. The woman also said that while Margaret Fischer and Jack Anderson were out of town away on business, Tanya should expect a callback from Ms. Fischer by the next day. "I have left her word of your concerns and I am sure she wouldn't want you to worry."

So even though she did not get any call from Chicago, she stalled because her luggage was light since her stuff was shipped ahead. Her phone was ringing regularly with everybody calling to give well wishes and goodbyes. She called Dr. Sullivan who has sent her a lovey journal to keep notes. She left her a message expressing how much she appreciated her caring gesture. Tanya went on to Africa as planned. She convinced herself that her fears were exaggerated, and she summoned up her trust in the process. She saw any retreat on her part as unjustified. This move had been a long time coming and there was no acceptable direction left to take, except straight ahead. So, with that, she boarded the flight for the first leg of her Africa-bound journey with a great

130 | JOBETH

sense of accomplishment and satisfaction for having cleared yet another milestone on the way to her new station in life.

****

Tanya's arrival at the Yaoundé Airport was much anticipated as she was warmly welcomed, even if her new community regarded her with some caution. She recognized the level of guardedness, even though she was regarded with respect. That was okay she was ready to build new relationships. She was carted off by her greeters to her small quarters in Doula. On the way, she took in the sights and sounds of their bumpy jaunt through the capital city of Yaoundé. As they passed through the noisy marketplace in Yaoundé, she was aware of the interesting way the locals looked at her. They knew what she would do and where she was going. They wondered about her personality.

Geyali, the friendly social worker that Dianna had spoken of, and another woman called Pangi, greeted her at the small brick structure that housed 4 apartments where Tanya would be staying. The women explained that they both lived there as well. They helped her with her things and led her to an apartment where Tanya saw the boxes, a little worse for wear, that she had shipped ahead from the States stacked up in a corner of the room that was one of two. The other room, obviously the bedroom, had a small cot. The bed was made. Pangi took credit for that. and explained that the local women made the quilts and pillows and had gladly sent them over for Tanya as a gift.

"How sweet! Thank you. Thank you. You have made me feel very welcome and all of the things I would be concerned about right away seem to be taken care of. I didn't know if

I would have to go get my things, but I see they are already here!"

"Geyali, I bring you greetings and hugs from Dianna. She misses you a great deal." The African woman smiled and put her hands together in a praying gesture.

"Bless her. I hope she is well. I miss her a great deal, as well." Geyali said.

Pangi said. "So, I will walk you over to the cafeteria so you can have some supper. You must be hungry. I hope you don't mind if I stop by the school to pick up my daughter, Kiki. She will go with us."

"Oh, no. I don't mind at all. Just let me wash up a bit." She looked around for the bathroom.

"Oh, down the hall we share the bath, toilet, and showers." Pangi pointed and Tanya grabbed her handbag and went in that direction.

"I will meet you outside then," she said over her shoulder as she went down the hall.

Tanya realized in the next few weeks that she was generally perceived as a Western woman who did everything too fast and spoke a little too loudly. The locals' experience had taught them to be patient with their American and European visitors. Most of the Westerners they knew were white people from France, Great Britain, and other European countries. For many of them, African Americans were an even more curious minority. Tanya would not begin to understand these dynamics until much later.

Language was not as big a problem as she had anticipated because most of the time there were English speakers in the hospitals and agencies she was engaged with. She learned that French was generally taught to children and most people spoke it, but she also found that the more highly educated people had also mastered English, which was taught in the secondary schools.

It turned out that the local Africans were as eager to understand her as she was to understand them. Their relationships were based on the exchange of goods and services and that was a strong motivation for both sides to become adept at using and manipulating the key lingo necessary to facilitate that relationship. She quickly learned the variations on certain words for health issues, education, food, and transportation that were needed to communicate clearly in each of the tribal dialects. It wasn't long before she began to get somewhat comfortable, at least enough to generally handle her daily business and affairs with some ease.

The culture and geography intrigued her. Of course, Dianna was right that life was much simpler than she was accustomed too. Accommodations and facilities were basic, and she realized after a few weeks that the access she had to running water and electricity was a cut above what most of the families she worked with were used to. Being in the city center near the hospital was an advantage. Still, she had to learn to tolerate dirt roads, dust, insects and not always being able to get water or the exact thing she wanted right at the time that she wanted it. Most of the time she wore her head wrapped with colorful swaths of fabric or floppy hats she bought from the market, in an attempt to protect her hair from the dust and insects.

The culture also had many blessings to appreciate. The people were more honest and more anecdotal. Dinner time was 'story time'. They listened to Kika's stories. Geyali and Pangi told stories to remember the past. They told the proverbs to teach lessons. On the weekends there was a lot of music and movement and dancing. Singing was a gift that so many of her new native community seemed to have been born with. It always seemed that they just automatically sounded well-practiced even when it came about spontaneously. The music added a more soulful atmosphere and the proverbs were wisdom that grounded the people in a communal experience..

Tanya was very aware that she was gradually becoming more relaxed. As a matter of fact, too much privacy was suspect. She discovered that she didn't need her customary defensive attitude in this new community. All of this learning and self-awareness was as valuable to the success of her work as conquering all of the language barriers. Africa was culturally and spiritually far from what she was familiar with. Further than she ever imagined.

She saw that the mission was not something she was creating from scratch. The social service compound in the center of Doula provided a combination of medical and social services through the various clinics and doctors. Nurses were highly trained and able to provide medical services and examination, Sometimes even performing minor procedures —and they were generally more available than the doctors. The Doula compound was a busy place where women sat nursing their babies and you could hear the coughing and cries of pain as people waited to be treated. The facility was a one stop center for the myriad needs of hundreds of people, and a loud symphony of discomfort filled the compound every day.

The primary school was also located in the compound and the sounds of children playing, singing, and reciting competed with the sounds of negotiating prices at the market, traffic, and even animal sounds from the goats, cattle, and chickens that came and went. Her office was located a short block away from the hospital. Wellness clinics sat between the primary school and the Red Cross, and across the road was a lively market where everything that women needed to carry out their responsibilities of keeping the homes, rearing young children, growing crops, and feeding their families, was sold.

Tanya related to the women as an educator and supporter and provided advice about programs that helped them become more efficient in their roles. She ran support groups and facilitated the formation of cooperative economic efforts. Her mission center ran various classes from sewing groups to soil and plant cultivation. Sometimes the women gathered to see educational movies on health issues, parenting or other related topics. Tanya networked with the Red Cross and other humanitarian, social and medical personnel to share information and bring in speakers of interest for her women's groups. She did what she could to elevate the women's literacy skills, and of course she provided Christian education through bible studies and regular worship service in bible stories, . It was challenging fun to help the young mothers and wives connect with biblical women like Rutha and Naomi, Esther, Lydia. Relating to women in the bible stories helped them as they worked through some of their own struggles with familial relationships and powerful government authorities.

Of course, her biggest professional challenge was getting young girls who were finishing primary school into the secondary schools, which were further away and not considered necessary for girls, especially by the male heads of their families. This area of her work was a challenge because, while she developed strong rapport with the women, she was not as connected to the men. The way the culture was structured men had more say as the children matured and advanced. It wasn't expected that females would be teachers or doctors, because it was common belief that females were destined to be wives and bear children. Their traditional roles were as wives and mothers, so as to strengthen their community and familial relations by marriage.

Tanya worked hard with the women who began to have more hopes for their girls, especially when they were bright and successful at school. They felt proud when their daughters received recognition for doing well and when they were recommended to attend the secondary schools. They would have been worried about the cost, but knew Tanya could make scholarships available. More education would make it possible for young girls to have a life beyond having babies and farming. The women were encouraged to dream as they became conscious of other possibilities. Tanya gave their newfound hopes and dreams voice and as the women became educated and strong, some of them became confident enough to advocate for their daughters' futures with their husbands within the family units. They became better able to put together convincing arguments that addressed the economic advantages of educating all of their children, not just the males. Tanya made them aware that these school placements also helped reduced the risks of their girls being exposed to HIV/AIDS by getting them out of the riskier rural areas where raping truckers and soldiers came through more and more often. Tanya had a small degree of success, but she didn't discount any of it. She felt that the enrollment of girls in secondary schools would increase as she continued to build relationships and that the benefits would increase over time.

All day on Wednesdays and on Saturday mornings the doctors came into the clinics. On those days there were more women around, and Tanya made every effort to connect with those mothers who had girls in the sixth and seventh levels of the primary school. She stood near the corner where women lined up with their small children and waited to see the doctors and handed out flyers to promote higher learning for girls. She chatted with the women she knew and introduced herself to others. She was a favorite with the children who quickly came to like her, and she gave out stickers and pencils with small fuzzy animals attached. She was greeted with hugs by the children, and she became quite an attraction.

One Wednesday by lunchtime she was exhausted and headed over to the cafeteria on the first floor of the hospital where the nurses, social workers, and doctors went to eat. While she was on the line getting her food, she was addressed by a doctor she had not met before.

"You are quite popular around here I see. I saw you playing with the children earlier."

"Oh, that is part of my job, I guess." She laughed.

"I don't think we have met." The young doctor reached for a roll as they moved along the buffet. "I'm Adam Sinclair. I just started working here at the wellness clinic and doing my rotation here at the hospital last week. I'm from London."

""No. We haven't met. I'm Tanya Stokes from New Jersey, in the United States." She replied.

"It's very nice to meet you, Tanya. I know I would much prefer to eat my lunch with you than alone. Do you mind?"

"No," she said hesitantly. She was immediately sorry she had agreed to sit with him. His accent was indeed British which sounded odd coming from him because she had not met many black men from England. He looked to be about her age and pleasant enough, but she just didn't feel her brain was functioning very well in the moment.

After that day, Adam and Tanya occasionally ate lunch together, but mostly she deliberately avoided him. Adam worked in the clinics on Wednesdays and Saturdays and also in the hospital several days a week. He was persistent about inviting her out, but it was a couple of months before she accepted an invitation to go on a real date with him to a movie and drinks in Yaoundé. Tanya went with him and realized she had not even thought about dating since she had come to Africa. She spent most of her spare time fixing up her quarters, writing fundraising letters, and studying languages. A couple of times she had accepted the invitation of the women to family celebrations and sometimes she had a night out with Pangi, Geyali and some of the other female workers and missionaries in the area, but mostly she worked and led quite a predictable and uneventful life. She secretly welcomed the chance to see more of the capital city and to be in the company of a man, socially. The movie they saw was an American one starring Michael Douglas. Afterwards they sat in an outdoor pub and drank a couple of beers as they chatted.

"So, tell me Tanya, what is a nice American girl like you doing so far away from home? I know what you do, but what brought you here?"

"Looking for adventure, I guess. I wanted to do something that seemed more meaningful. Just felt like I needed to get out of my comfort zone. What about you?"

"Well, I just wanted to see another part of the world and get some experience. My father is a doctor and has an office in London. I don't know, it just seemed like a death sentence to spend all those years getting my medical degree and then

138 | JOBETH

just go into that office and there be nothing else. I wanted adventure too, I guess, just like you, Tanya."

"And I bet there is some little lady eagerly awaiting your return." Tanya quickly covered her mouth with her hand. "I am so sorry. I shouldn't have said that. Just in the states doctors are sought after…considered a good catch."

"Actually, there is a little lady right here that I am very enamored with. I wonder what she thinks of me."

Tanya was caught off guard by his comment. "Well now…I think you are impressive. And I am enjoying spending the evening with you."

* * * * * * * * *

Flirting and having to deal with the attention of a man was scary for Tanya. She was not all that secure with the kind of shaky proposition a romantic relationship was. She had remained dutiful about keeping up with her program at least via computer even with her transcontinental travel. She had continued to read and reflect on the 12 step program principles she depended on for maintaining her sanity and safety from the destructive tendencies she had succumbed to in the past. She knew how much the addict in her would love to drive a wedge between her and her sanity, but she was proud of maintaining her commitment to overcoming her addictions. It was one thing to write, reflect and think about principles, but with Adam's presence in her life, she saw that she was required to apply the theories she had only thought about up until then. She wondered if she could live up to that commitment, as she guarded her tongue and was careful not to start manufacturing fantasies. In fact, the first few times after their initial meeting she was worried about any interaction with him at all. She felt she was at a distinct disadvantage, so far away from home and the sponsors and mentors who had helped her in the past.

Up till now, she had kept to her work and cultivated very few social alliances beside those of her housemates, Geyali and Pangi. Both Tanya and Pangi relied on Geyali for a closer connection to and understanding of the new culture around them. Since Geyali was the Director of the Women's Center she was Tanya's boss, but Geyali always related more as a sage and a comrade, as a co-worker. After their introductions Tanya felt nothing but equality with and respect for Geyali. She understood immediately why Dianna would have kept her relationship with this woman and she knew she would try to do the same. Geyali was director of the Women's Center because she was wise in all ways, with regard to the population there in Cameroon and she was sincere and well-respected.

The first few times Adam asked Tanya out she had made up excuses to refuse him. She talked herself into passing up on what might be an opportunity to be the girlfriend of the newest 'hot prospect" in the compound. She was keenly aware that in another time and place she would have immediately begun to manipulate that situation within the first couple of days of Adam's arrival. As it were, she kept to herself a lot and chided herself for even thinking about the possibility. She was always careful to keep a steady exchange of correspondence going with Elva and Rochelle, so that she would stay in touch with where she had come from. She felt it was important to remember her past, so she did not repeat the same mistakes. She clearly remembered what the psychologist had said to her during her psychological evaluation for call that the last thing Tanya wanted was to

140 | JOBETH

get caught up in anything in Africa that proved more than she could handle.

Dear Tanya:

I was so glad to hear from you. I'm glad to know you're well and that you're enjoying your work in the Motherland. I am also very glad to know that you remain conscious and sober! You are right that your biggest test to date is now in front of you. In walks Adam! The most important thing is to realize, that you are just fine already. Don't start crazy making! There is nothing you need from anyone, not this Adam guy, or anyone else – not to complete you. Nothing does that – not love, not sex, not anything! Don't believe the things you remember hearing on the radio and in poetry all our lives. You are living well, lady! Any relationship you develop should not be a drain or a pain.

Now having said that, know that whenever you think about a relationship it should be about a level of spiritual joy is all. Think about what we have to offer each other beyond physical gratification, otherwise there is no point. Please remember you are too precious to waste yourself at all. Nobody says you have to be a hermit - that is not your goal at all. You should be able to enjoy yourself – to laugh, to dance and to hope - without giving up your self-respect and dignity. Sex should never come into the picture until mutual respect is established as real - the real thing between two people.

Love you, Elva

P.S. I hope you can come home soon. You have been gone long enough!

* * * * * * * * *

PART SIX
Finding Shalom

The sun rose high in the sky over the compound each morning summoning the livestock first, so Tanya's slumber was disturbed by the roosters crowing and the clucking of chickens. If that wasn't enough, she could hear the call, Adhan, because here Islam was the professed and practiced faith of many people. The call was a beautiful sound in the fresh dark morning echoing over the speakers. The Adhan was majestic in its tone of authority, and it drew an assured and reverent response. The people were up early and long before dawn, you could hear the shuffling of feet on the dirt roads and the procession of people going to prayer, going to work and getting about the business of the came to highly regard her new neighbors for their character. When she awoke to the Adhan she knew her friend Pangi had already gone to join her Muslim brothers and sisters making *salat.*

Tanya had her morning rituals. Upon waking she would do her meditations and sit with her Bible. She savored those early hours of reading and prayer. She included in her prayers her community in Africa and at home. She also said special prayers for her daughter Mia, who she only spoke to about once a month and otherwise communicated with through short emails and letters. She enumerated the concerns of her women's groups and their particular problems... praying about their separation from family members and their grief for their lost relatives, their men at war, their living children and their unborn children. She prayed God help them and that aid would be forthcoming from the human community as well.

When she finished her devotional time, she would fix cereal and coffee, (tea for Pangi) and wait for Pangi to return. When Pangi arrived with her head wrapped loosely with a large scarf, the day began. They ate together and discussed workshop plans before Pangi went off to carry out her nursing duties at the clinic and the hospital. They planned workshops about health, safety, and childcare. It had become clear that both the spiritual and physical health of the women needed to be addressed in whatever they did. In order to educate and empower the women they had to take a holistic approach. Concerns included a vast array of antiquated, traditional views about sexuality, womanhood, marriage and childcare. When Tanya and Pangi collaborated, Tanya brought her foundation in spirituality to bear while Pangi, who was revered as a "doctor", brought in the health-related concerns. They became an effective team and were enjoying a high degree of success with their efforts. When they led sessions together, they instinctively gauged when it was the best time for one or the other to respond or to address an issue as it came up.

Kiki, Pangi's young daughter, attended the primary school during the day and trailed Pangi and Tanya during the evenings. At 8 years old she was quite independent and would sit in the offices and meeting rooms doing her homework and studying and when that was done, she would play games outside with other children. She knew all of the languages and had grown up in the compound, so she helped the constant influx of new children to adapt. She was a junior ambassador of sorts in the community and was well-respected and valued by children and adults. Tanya ran many activities and movies for the children and often Kiki would attend. Pangi didn't mind that some of these activities were Christian. She didn't think it mattered most of the time, and she was sure Kiki knew the difference because Pangi had studied Quran with her daughter from a young age. Occasionally, when Kiki asked a faith-based question, either Tanya or Pangi would need to clarify. Tanya regularly invited Kiki and other Muslim children to explain Muslim beliefs or practices to the rest of the group during youth gatherings. She hoped this sharing fostered a deep respect for the religious differences between them.

As time went on Tanya continued to date Adam Sinclair, meeting him for lunch a few times a week and their relationship was developing further. He afforded her ample opportunities to venture beyond the confines of the village compound and he was a lot more familiar with tourist attractions and activities than she was. He took her to an Anglican Church once and they would find moments to steal away for a stroll or to grab supper together. One weekend Adam took her to the beach along the Atlantic coast and she was glad to see the ocean for the first time since she had been in Africa. Her time with Adam was always a welcome departure from her normal routine of evening meals with Pangi and Kiki, which were usually eaten in the hospital cafeteria. Once or twice the ladies went into Yaoundé and they walked around taking in the sights and shopping, and then ended the day with special culinary treats. Kiki was delighted to get her favorite peanut butter candy and they would buy sweet oranges to take back home.

When Pangi had been Kiki's age, her father taught her that she was a princess, which meant she was naturally destined to be a queen. It was all laid out in some kind of strategic plan from on high. Pangi was draped in silk and gold and given her every desire. Her father laid out a path before her like an ornate carpet that led to some high place where she would be seated at the head next to her betrothed king. But somewhere along the way, as Pangi encountered those who were less fortunate, her gaze turned away from the vision of such a dazzling future. She had a loving heart and a giving nature, rather than an ambitious desire for personal gain. She may have been seen as rebellious in the context of Eastern

146 | JOBETH

immigrant ideals, but she was being guided by her spiritual compass that led her further and further away from a forced paternalistic fantasy of light reflecting off tinkling gems and the noise of contrived trumpet flourish. Her true self was not nearly so glamorous. She never saw herself as princess material.

* * * * * * * * *

As it turned out, Geyali's warnings were not unwarranted. It was becoming increasingly obvious that people were fleeing from the fighting of the militias up north and seeking refuge in Doula, as well as Yaoundé and other cities in the region where they could find services and accommodations. For Tanya, Pangi, Geyali, Adam and their coworkers that meant more rape cases, more malaria cases, more cases of HIV/AIDS, and more people with hunger related issues and injuries. Their fragile social service apparatus was struggling under the pressure to meet the needs of the influx of refugees. Tanya's work became more focused on responding to social crises than on education and enrichment as the crises mounted. For the workers in the compound the processing of incoming refugees into convents or makeshift camps, organizing the camps, and seeing that the hungry were fed, were tasks no less important than taking care of medical needs.

Tanya frequently checked the bulletins posted on the internet and listened to the daily reports from the Embassy about the encroaching violence. Margaret Fischer was in touch with her by email and was talking in terms of possible evacuation. From Fischer, Tanya was receiving instructions and contact information for officials at the embassy who were handling travel arrangements for American citizens. She could no longer delude herself about the seriousness of the situation.

Geyali, Pangi, and Tanya sat around on the porch in front of their complex one night. The warm air was permeated with a mixture of organic human and animal smells, but still, it was calm and quiet at that hour. That was something to appreciate because in that moment they could allow their tired aching bodies to rest.

"What will happen to us all?" was the unspoken question that hung in the air all around them. Day by day they were living and breathing a truckload of pestilence and uncertainty.

Geyali was resigned, as she sat on the wooden fence that framed the porch. Tanya sat in a wicker settee and pretended to be unperturbed. Pangi had her back to both of them facing out toward the village that spread out in front of them.

"I don't think I'll be here much longer. I have to protect Kiki if I can. Things don't look so good. It is one thing to make choices for myself, but it's not fair for me to sacrifice my daughter." Pangi's thick black curly hair was pulled back and gathered into a band and her deep-set dark eyes focused on something far off in the distance. The day's sweat and grime were settled in the lines that drew her beautiful face.

"I hear you. I think of leaving too, but when I do, I feel like I would be abandoning the people here who are depending on us." Tanya responded to Pangi. There was silence.

"This place is trouble," Geyali added thoughtfully, after a while, with her native wisdom. "That is the way it is. You can't stop this trouble. It was trouble before you and after you, it will be trouble still."

"I know. You are right, Geyali. I came to help, but it's hard to make a difference in a war zone …" Pangi had a lot at stake with an eight-year-old daughter to think about. She was a Pakistani American and had grown up the only daughter of her father who had done well in the import business providing goods from Eastern venues to supply American markets catering to growing immigrant communities. His financial success supported a comfortable life for his wife and family and a good education for Pangi who excelled in her studies. Pangi had a sharp mind and a work ethic that reflected her parent's values. She was receptive to science and mathematics and became interested in medicine. She had decided at college to go into nursing. Her mother and father had expected her to marry and bear children, but that was not what happened. Pangi had a caring nature and the same humanitarian spirit that led her to nursing led her to spend a year in the U.S. Peace Corp. Her experience working with the Peace Corps for a year had taken her to Egypt. Growing up she had taken regular excursions to Pakistan with her family and as a result of her exposure to the developing world, she gained a heightened awareness of the prevailing needs of people outside of the U.S. Upon completing her studies, Pangi's background, made working with the Red Cross as a health worker in Africa a suitable fit, especially with the HIV pandemic exploding during the 80's. She became part of the legion of helping hands who dedicated themselves to lending support to lessen the impact of a disease that threatened to annihilate an already fragile humanity.

Pangi had been working in Africa for two years when she met Abina, Kiki's mother, who was one of the women she helped to care for. Kiki's mother lived long enough to share with Pangi that she was not only HIV positive, but also victimized by rape. The stigma of her situation had left her abandoned by her husband and scorned by her village community. It wasn't long before Abina succumbed to the virus, and her death left a two-year-old Kiki orphaned. Pangi took over caring for Kiki as it was the most natural thing in the world for her to do. The original plan was to put Kiki in the system that would have placed her with hordes of other children in the same predicament, but Pangi loved Kiki and adopted her. Although she didn't follow her parent's expectations, she became a mother still. Kiki never lived in America, but now Pangi thought that maybe that time was coming with the encroaching chaos all around. For six years she had mothered her little girl in her native country. Maybe it was time for Kiki to go to America.

Every day people were leaving. It became clear that if you had a choice you needed to get out while you could. The soldiers didn't come into the compound and the UN guards kept up a lively presence around them as a deterrent. Of course, the threat was always there that the soldiers would lay hold of them and completely tear down their community. As it were from all reports, the warlords besieged the homes, land, and resources the refugees left behind. Resting and gorging on their spoils they sustained their murderous selves. There was no way to know when the warring soldiers would exhaust their stolen resources and attempt to avail their ravenous appetite of the humanitarian relief that the compounds made available. It had come to the point that the people no longer cared about their warring but only wanted it to stop because anyway you looked at it, it was not desirable to destroy the whole world.

Adam Sinclair was looking ragged and dusty in his rickety jeep as he rode up alongside Tanya. Tanya was always busy, it seemed, and they had not seen much of each other lately. She was carrying a basket of supplies from the commissary to one of the camp areas. He waved at her to let her know he wanted to talk to her.

"Hey there!"

"Hey there, yourself!" she said as she got closer.

"What do you have there?" he said, adding quickly, "I sure miss you."

"Yes. Me too. It's just been hectic around here...just now carrying some supplies over to nurses down the road."

"I see. Look, I know there is always something to do, but I would like to steal you away briefly. I want to talk to you about some things."

"What's on your mind?" she queried.

"Come ride with me. I'll tell you on the way. I was going to pick up the post. Come go with me...it won't be long."

Tanya looked up at the scorching sun and wiped her brow. "I could use a break, I guess. Take me to drop off this basket first and I'll go with you."

When they got on the road, she noticed how tired and worn out Adam looked, and she guessed she didn't look much better. She tried to straighten her straw hat and tuck her stray locks under it.

He noticed her primping. "You're beautiful, even now. How are you faring?"

"It's difficult and my church is urging me to come home."

"Yes, it is about that time. That is what I wanted to talk to you about. I am going to be returning to London very shortly."

"Really? I hadn't thought of you leaving, but I can't say I am surprised. It seems that every day we are saying goodbye."

"That is true. I hate to say that the situation here is hopeless, but it is. It is time. I feel it in my bones. The jig is up, so to speak. But YOU. I feel we have unfinished business."

Tanya was looking right at his lips moving, but she couldn't quite figure out what to say.

He kept talking. "I don't feel good about leaving you here. I had hoped…" His voice trailed off.

"I guess we have hardly gotten to know each other, and things just went awry. She furrowed her brow as she shrugged her shoulders. "There has been no time."

"No. You're right. But Tanya, we can have all the time we want. I sometimes imagine you and me somewhere else - making a go of it. I can see myself married to you, having children, and all of that."

"Oh Adam, you are not being realistic. You are a great guy but…I can't think…well, don't get me wrong! I mean, I just cannot think straight out here, in this jungle, with all hell breaking loose."

"I know…I know… but listen, I am not leaving until next week. Won't you think about it?"

"Think about what?"

"Think about coming home with me." He was looking all wild-eyed.

"Adam, are you crazy? I am an American! I have a home and you are asking… well, a lot… and very quickly! I just feel all tangled up with this," she waved her hands in the air. "With the church, with everything! I have a family back home…my daughter…"

Adam interrupted her. "I know all these things, but you are free, Tanya. Free to do whatever you want…believe it or not.

We can travel to and fro and be in contact with your family." He stopped talking and stopped the jeep in the middle of the road. He leaned over and gave her a long, lingering kiss. "Won't you just say you will think about it? It is a heavy load that I have dumped on you…but please, think about it. I have never met anyone like you, and I don't think I will ever again. Will you do me the courtesy of just thinking about it…you and me?"

"I will think about it," she murmured softly as she was still stunned by it all.

* * * * * * * * *

Tanya and Adam continued their run to the post office at the embassy. When they got there the grounds were almost deserted. As a result of the recent displacement and upheaval of the population, there was very little activity around. Tanya, still shaken, from Adam's revelations and requests, decided to stay in the car. She needed a moment to try to put her thoughts in order. She hadn't expected Adam to come on so strongly and she certainly hadn't expected a marriage proposal. The picture he painted was not something she had imagined. While she liked Adam a lot and felt she would miss him immensely, still she didn't feel she was "in love" with him. Sure, he was a doctor, and some people would think that was a good thing, but Tanya had never been to England at all, and moving there to make a life with Adam just seemed far-fetched. The more she thought about it, or rather "felt it" in her gut, it just wasn't right. She knew already without thinking it through any further, that marrying Adam just felt all wrong. She was not even ready to go steady, let alone get married!

On the way back to the compound they were quiet.

"Well, I hope you are thinking about me," Adam said after they rode in silence for a while.

Tanya didn't want to be rude to him, "You know that I am…" she murmured as they moved along.

"I am sorry too, that all this is coming to an end." She looked around, taking in the view of the dirt road, and the trees, as she listened to nature's soundtrack of birds, insects, frogs, and monkeys. What was so loud and distracting a few months ago had become familiar. "I will so miss all this, no matter what happens next."

"It is a beautiful place. I hope it survives these times…that it will all be here later."

They rode along slowly, knowing this might be the last time they got to do this together. A tear escaped Tanya's left eye and rolled down her cheek. She didn't want Adam to see her crying, so she bent forward, using her handkerchief to wipe her face and neck. Just then she heard a sound like a coo, followed by a whimper. She stopped wiping and held her head up, her nose in the air. "Did you hear that?"

"No. What?" Adam answered. Tanya placed her hand on his chest and held up her left hand. Adam stopped the jeep. Just then they both heard a child's voice whining softly. Tanya wondered who would be out here in the trees. She had not seen anybody walking on the road, but now she distinctly heard a child.

"Helloooo…who's there?" She called out in English, then in French. They began to hear someone moving, a rustling in the bushes. And then she saw him…a beautiful baby boy. He was brown like coffee beans, and he had big watery, dark eyes. He was wrapped in a rice cloth and wearing sandals.

His hair was bushy and curly, and his face was wet with tears and the mucous from his runny nose. His distress became a smile as he saw Tanya's face.

"What's going on here?" Adam was behind her, as they both looked around expecting an adult to appear, but the boy who looked to be about two years old seemed to be alone. Adam decided to walk about and see if there was someone in the area who might be responsible for the child. Tanya stayed with the boy and was cautious to talk softly to him; careful not to touch him, so he would not be frightened. He was afraid and tired, and she got the feeling he was glad to have been discovered.

Maybe he had been sleeping and their jeep passing had awakened him. There were leaves and twigs in his hair. Suddenly he started to sway slightly and then he collapsed to the ground. Tanya shook him gently and when he started to come to, she ran and got her water bottle out of the car and cradled him to offer him water. He drank a good portion of it, only stopping to catch his breath and to look around to see if anyone else was coming. He remained somewhat listless.

Adam returned after about 10 minutes to find Tanya sitting on the ground rocking the boy. "There is no one else in the area. I guess they could have meant to come back for him?" He looked puzzled.

"Well, I don't want to leave him here. He is hungry and thirsty. I don't think he is well. Besides, it will be dark soon. Who knows what could happen to him if we leave him here?" Tanya responded. He seemed to be falling asleep.

"You are right about that. Maybe he got lost from his family…they may be up in the camps looking for him."

"You know you are probably right. I say let's take him up there and I am sure someone will come looking for him eventually. Surely they'll look at the camp."

That was how Tanya met Asmar. She would later call him that, because in Swahili, *Asmar* means brown skin.

Nobody came to get Asmar. Tanya felt she was the only one who cared about him. In Tanya's mind, it was no accident, that when she had decided to leave Cameroon, their paths had crossed. Her life was changing, and she didn't have a plan, but fortunately, God always seemed to have one for her. As surprising as it was, the good Lord's plans for Asmar and Tanya seemed intertwined. Although her Africa experience was ending, she was not headed for high society in London. Maybe her Africa experience was not truly ending, but only continuing in an unexpected maternal way.

Adam Sinclair examined the boy and ran some tests to assess his health. To their relief, he was not carrying the AIDS virus. He did have an extreme case of anemia which was no surprise. Somewhere else in the world, the severity of the boy's anemic condition would have involved a regimen of iron supplements and dietary programming. Without an adequate supply of reliable supplements, the doctor opted for a blood transfusion to immediately improve the quality of the boy's blood. Pangi had banked blood for her daughter, in case of an emergency and some of that blood was given to Asmar, as it was discovered that Asmar and Kiki had the same blood type.

For a foreigner, adopting an African child is not the easiest thing to do. As Tanya began to inquire about the process, she found that the organizations that handled international adoptions, as well as the African government, had concerns about the loss of culture that is at risk in international adoptions. In Tanya's case, the fact that she was African American worked in her favor. Finally, she had to agree to live in Cameroon with Asmar for at least six months before she could take him out of the country. That seemed reasonable to her, if not all that convenient.

After Adam had helped her with Asmar, the doctor went forward with his preparations to leave. They spent an emotional and rather rushed last meeting together in the clinic less than a week later. Tanya tried to explain that she certainly couldn't entertain marriage or a move to England because of the new developments with Asmar. They both knew that wasn't the real reason, but they accepted the fact that no further cementing of their status as a couple was ever going to happen.

"I just can't do that. The timing is all off! But Adam you have been the most wonderful friend through these months, and I will never forget you. If I am ever in England, I will look you up, for sure."

He looked at her with sadness in his eyes. "I hope you will, Tanya..." Searching her face he said softly. "My fantastic woman, whom I will never forget..." He backed up and cleared his throat. "Sooo... I should be getting on." She rushed to embrace him for a moment and then she left.

Soon Geyali, Pangi, and Tanya were also saying their goodbyes the night before they were all headed for the airport and their respective destinations. Gayali pulled out some beer she had saved for a special occasion.

"It is a good time to share this. My warrior sisters who have done so much for the people will be missed, but I know you will do good things wherever you go." They all raised their bottles, sipped, and then placed them down on the bare table in the center of Tanya's room.

Tanya looked around at their luggage and the bags, all stacked up. Kiki and Asmar were fast asleep in sleeping bags in Pangi's apartment down the hall, where all of their bed rolls were laid out for this last night.

"Geyali…we would have been lost without you. You have been more than a wonderful colleague, but a guide and a mentor and I will always appreciate that." Tanya said.

"That is so true. I remember when I got Kiki; I would not have stayed here were it not for your support. So, you will go to your sister's place…and then what?" Pangi asked.

"Yes, she is waiting for me, and we will have a lot of catching up to do. I will miss my work here but on to the next thing! Nobody knows." Geyali said. She paused thoughtfully and then she said, "The children…they are brother and sister. Do you know that? They have the same blood."

"Who? You mean Kiki and Asmar?" Tanya was puzzled. Her eyes met Pangi's across the table. "I guess you are right, in a way, with the blood and all."

"That is not the only thing. Don't you see? Look at the head. Look at the eyes." She chuckled and shook her head. "The feet; the hair. Same genes."

Pangi said. "That is ridiculous, Geyali, AND impossible. Abina is dead. She was dead by the time Kiki was 2."

"Still, they are family. Here we know. We see the ancestors in them, the family connection."

"Okay, Geyali. If you say so, I don't guess we can prove you wrong." Tanya and Pangi were equally intrigued by the idea. Only three weeks had passed since they had met Asmar. It was hard to believe that Pangi and Kiki were going home to New Jersey and Tanya had arranged to take a position

158 | JOBETH

with a convent settlement that was willing to let her bring Asmar into the community. Her brain was on overload, as well as her heart. She could not take Geyali seriously, in that moment, because there was too much going on in her head already. She hated saying goodbye to her and Pangi. Kiki had indeed been Asmar's big sister for that little while, and at the airport, they hugged for a long time and solemnly exchanged their 'pet rocks with one another. Kiki took the one that said **Asmar,** and he took hers with her name on it.

* * * * * * * * * *

The mission settlement in the hills of Cameroon had been run by the Sisters of St. Bernadette for more than 100 years. Influenced by the Mennonites, the mission existed to evangelize and educate indigenous African masses in the faith and mores of an enlightened Mennonite culture and spirituality. Their efforts had produced an impressive teaching university and a mission day school. As Tanya took advantage of the opportunity to begin her studies toward a teaching degree at the university, she also enjoyed her job of tutoring a group of youth completing their courses at the day school. Child care was provided for the children of staff members, so this was an ideal place in terms of Tanya's particular situation. Such a curious blend of academia, youthful presence of children, and the pastoral made her feel like she had passed into some parallel existence that was such a contrast to the hard world she had been living in.

The children Tanya tutored were of the age when authority was respected, and learning was worthy. She was given responsibility for eight 10- and 11-year-olds to drill in the humanities and classics according to a strict curriculum. There was no deviating from the proscribed course of instruction. In this system, failure was seen to be as much the fault of the teaching as the learning.

This sharp detour that her career had taken was the result of a month of hurried letter-writing on her part. She had written to everyone from immediate family members to extended family members and friends, and from the New Jersey bishop to the Global Mission directors in Chicago. As a result of a flurry of mail and calls she had terminated her call to the women's organization in Cameroon and been placed on leave in good standing with the New Jersey Bishop's office. She had asked her bishop and the Global Mission directors for deferments on her speaking obligations while she completed the adoption. The Bishop was fascinated with her story and considered it so novel that he sent her a congratulatory note about the divine outcomes of her call.

Young Asmar was thriving and had adapted well to the new environment in the hillsides of Cameroon. He was happy with the stable environment and young enough to embrace new things easily. His health improved rapidly, and he and Tanya bonded well. They were like a healing salve for one another. By the time the six-month waiting period was up, Tanya was anxious to go home and share Asmar with her family and friends, and she was as anxious to see Pangi, as she was to see anybody.

The feelings were mutual, as she was greeted by a rowdy welcoming party that included her daughter, Mia, her mom, her sisters, her friend and confidante, Elva, and of course Pangi and Kiki. She was reminded of the warm welcome she had received upon arriving in Cameroon more than a year ago. She felt extremely blessed to be the recipient of so much goodwill on opposite sides of the globe. She was returning from a journey that was much more than geographic, so she wasn't sure she was the same person who had left the country all those months before. Tanya's recollection of that person was like a flimsy, filmy version of her new self. Now she was so much more vivid.

Asmar was a little stunned by the intensity of his new family, but he took his cues from Tanya's joyful demeanor. He could sense that all this excitement was a good thing for him and his mom, so he smiled and hugged and blushed appropriately.

"He is such a moocher!" Tanya said as she saw how Asmar lovingly stroked Mia's face, who was holding him with puckered lips, and planting as many kisses as she could manage on his round brown face. They were both spirited away by their greeters amidst local news updates and reports and ideas for things to do together -- just as it should be.

* * * * * * * * *

Kiki's and Pangi's arrival in the US had not been so joyously welcoming. Kiki had never experienced any kind of train ride or an airport, so the tram that carried them from the terminal to the security checkpoint was amazing to her. There was so much and so many different kinds of people to see. She never had much experience beyond the social service compound in Cameroon and what it offered. For an eight-year-old, her knowledge of language, religion, and ethnicity was broader than American children her age. She also had an advantage coming into the US because she knew English already so the language didn't present a barrier. However, in other ways, her experience was very limited. Nothing had prepared her for the urban American experience or a consumer society on such a grand scale. Commuter transportation, shopping malls, entertainment, and so much advanced technology were a culture shock for her, and she was delighted to indulge in and experience it. Pangi had been away long enough to notice a certain degree of technological advance that was new to her, but she had a much closer point of reference than Kiki did. She understood the advantages America afforded, but she also wanted to shield her daughter from too much, too fast, because she knew those advantages could be harmful too. There was a part of her that lamented the inevitable dissolution of Kiki's purity and innocence.

Pangi had managed to keep her family in the dark about Kiki. She always felt it was better to wait until she came home to explain things. It was easier to put her hope in her past experience of a loving and adoring family. Omar Abassi met her at the airport. He was dressed in formal attire as was Pangi because as she had suspected, an elaborate feast of welcoming was waiting for her at her parents' home. Kiki was happy to dress up for the party as well. Of course, they were dripping with the jewelry that was meant to be worn for such celebratory occasions and Pangi had not forgotten how to make up accordingly.

When Omar Abassi laid eyes on his daughter at the terminal his eyes danced with joy and his smile was so broad it was as if it would burst his face open and he felt a sense of peace in his chest that made him aware of how much he had worried about Pangi over the years. Her absence had been hard to explain to his brothers and family, but now that she was home things could take their normal course and the unusual departure from tradition could be forgotten. He was certainly willing to forget, it because now things could be set properly in place.

After they exchanged their greetings Pangi looked for her mother somewhere nearby.

162 | JOBETH

"Where is mom?"

"Oh no, she is at home. She is preparing the feast, of course. Everything must be just so, for our long-gone princess. She has been going on for weeks!" He was waving his arms about to indicate Nur Abassi's flurry of activity.

He added. "Not a wedding… but still, you have come home! Who knows what can happen next!" He was laughing, with a teasing wink.

"Come let us hurry!" He was taking charge. "Your baggage? I have a car waiting."

"Yes. Of course." Pangi said. Just then, Pangi felt Kiki tugging on her brocade-encrusted wrap that hung low and wide and had been providing a protective place for a shy girl to hide until her mom attempted to adjust it, as she handed off their carry-on bags to Omar.

"I see you have a traveling companion!" Omar was surprised as he suddenly became aware of the young girl's presence. The decibels of brightness on his face were immediately turned down and a look of mild puzzlement came like a shadow across his face. "And who is this?"

"Father, please, meet Kiki! Say hello, Kiki. This is my father. Remember, I told you about him?"

Kiki smiled with her head down and put her hand to her mouth holding one finger over her lips as she peeked out from under Pangi's flowing attire.

"Hello, Kiki." Omar was still bewildered as he looked down at the little girl. Now he looked around and past Pangi. "And where are your parents, little one?"

Pangi knew this was not the time or the place to try to set him straight. She chuckled nervously. "Kiki is from Cameroon,

Papa. She is a little shy, but let's get our things and be on our way. We have had such a long journey." She quickly turned her back to her father, grabbed Kiki's hand, and began walking toward the baggage claim area. Omar watched her walk away, shocked for a moment, by his daughter's seemingly abrupt dismissal.

"Can you get a cart for us?" Pangi was saying over her shoulder.

"Yes, yes," Omar answered, regaining his composure somewhat, as he turned to find assistance.

From that point on, the mood was changed. Omar could see he had been put off by Pangi and he still had questions. He was used to being in charge, and he was feeling ill-equipped, as they started the ride to his home. He was uninformed and that annoyed him. How could he answer the questions his brothers would have when they got to the house or even those of his wife?

"So, you are well?" He asked after they had road along awhile.

"Yes. Very well, thank you. And you look healthy, Papa. How is Mom? I hope she is not overexerting herself with this party. It is not necessary."

"Hah! *You* try to tell her that." He made an effort to lighten the mood. "She is so happy and so proud of our little world traveler. She must show you off to the world."

When they got to the house there was so much excitement, Pangi didn't have to do much beyond introductions all around with Kiki at first. The brothers, the cousins, some neighbors, and friends were all there making a fuss over her. Kiki was not the focus of their attention although knowing glances made it clear she was not going unnoticed. Pangi and Kiki were allowed to use the bathroom and freshen up in the

164 | JOBETH

bedroom, but it wasn't long before Nur Abassi was knocking at the door, obviously sent by Omar to get the scoop.

"So, who is this little lady you have brought home with you, my dear Pangi?"

"She is my daughter, Mom. I have adopted her, and she has been my daughter for several years, now." Pangi was a matter of fact.

"You cannot be serious! How can you just adopt an African child? Do you know what you have done?" Her mother did not look happy.

Pangi looked at Kiki sitting on a chair by the bedroom window. The girl looked concerned. Pangi placed her hand on her mother's shoulder for a second and then went over to Kiki. She squatted down and said to the girl. "Kiki why don't you go into the bathroom and wash your face and hands, okay? Here are your toiletries." She handed her a small case. She walked quickly to the door and guided her mom into the hall.

"Mom I love this little girl and her mother is dead." She explained.

"Okay, then we will find her a suitable home. Of course." Her mother said.

"Mom! I adopted her! She is staying with me. She is mine. I am keeping her."

Nur looked at Pangi as if her skin had turned green. She was having a hard time making sense of the situation. This new development just did not fit into any of the plans she had been discussing with her husband and her relatives. Nobody she knew would be able to accept Pangi into their family with this Kiki.

"Pangi, have you gone mad? She is not even Pakistani. What about marriage…"

"Mom. I am not worried about that right now. Kiki is my main concern and that is all there is to it."

Nur was crying now. She looked panic-stricken. "Pangi, do you know what this means? Do you know what you are doing? You are destroying your father. You are destroying our family!"

Pangi realized her mother was right. She realized now that her father was standing at the bottom of the stairs looking up at them and he had the same panic-stricken look in his eyes that her mother had, only her mother's face was wet with tears and his jaw was set in stone. He looked right at her and he turned and walked away.

After that initial meeting, Kiki never saw the grandparents again. Her father would not speak to Pangi at all. They stayed for dinner, but Omar stayed in the library and refused to come out. Kiki was disappointed and confused because these grandparents didn't seem anything like the parents her mom had described to her over the years. They didn't like her and that didn't feel good. Her mom said not to worry about them, that they didn't know her. She told her they would be getting their own house and she would have a wonderful life in America. Pangi was sorry she had brought Kiki there, not to America, but to her parents to be rejected.

"I love you plenty, Kiki." She told the girl on their way to a hotel that night. "Allah loves you and you just need to love yourself. That is all that matters. We will be fine." Kiki fell asleep as she nestled under her mother's arm feeling the warm vibration that rippled in her mom's body as she spoke to her. This was the love she had always known, and she was just fine.

****

There was no way that Tanya return to the same living situation at Lord of Life, where she had been living temporarily before her world tours began, not with a young child to care for. She would be forever grateful to the pastors, John Warren and David Black, for their concern and generosity, but her needs had grown substantially. In the time since they had left Cameroon, Pangi's life had taken some unpredictable turns, as well. The Abbasi family had not been forthcoming in embracing Pangi's blissful maternal state and had virtually disowned her. Their hopes that the magnanimous leniency they had extended to their daughter would have caused Pangi to accept her ancestral heritage of nobility were ended when she returned to America with the African child. They could not accept Kiki as their own and felt compelled to shun Pangi, as well. Her situation was seen as shameful and made her unsuitable to mate with a proper Abbasi descendant. Her father's dismissal of her was swift and Pangi's mother understood she was childless from that point on. Pangi had feared all those years in Africa that for all of her father's adoration of her, his love had impenetrable limits. Now she knew she had been right to keep Kiki overseas for so long and why she had savored her relationship and communication with her mother during those years. She had known on some level that their relationship would be over. She began to prepare to make her way and moved forward to purchase a home that would be suitable for a family that she envisioned for herself on her own terms.

Pangi had written to Tanya while her friend was in residence at the Mennonite settlement and was glad to have her encouragement as she faced the harshness of her return home. For her and Kiki, Tanya and Asmar were the family they felt connected to and loved by, more than any other. It seemed to make sense for all concerned for Pangi to invite Tanya to bring Asmar to stay with her and Kiki, at least, until Tanya could sort out her affairs. Tanya accepted the invitation. The home Pangi purchased was a two-story cottage in a rustic suburban area in northern New Jersey. Tanya was a city girl through and through, so Pangi's quarters nestled among the maple and oak trees set back off the road seemed like the hinterlands, as far as she was concerned. On the other hand, it was beautiful and clean and Pangi and Kiki were there.

"Mia gave me all your mail. It is in a box there in the hall." Pangi said as they walked in the door and plopped down luggage and bags.

Kiki and Asmar went running up the stairs. Kiki ran up as Asmar followed navigating the stairs as quickly as he was able with his short legs.

Kiki was saying: "I will show you your room. Wait until you see what we got for you!"

Tanya peeked into the dining room and peered into the living room and the downstairs bedroom.

While Pangi was hanging coats in the closet, she said. "Make yourself at home and I will put on some coffee and tea. Are you hungry? I am starved! I will make some sandwiches."

Tanya sat in the kitchen at the counter while Pangi prepared the meal. They caught up on more of the developments of the last few months. Pangi called the children down and they took their lunches off into the den. She and Tanya sat at the dining room table and continued their conversation.

"This is awesome, Pangi. I like the house. It is so big. Are you happy here?" Tanya said.

"I am very happy here. I didn't plan it this way, of course. I had some unreasonable hopes of being tied in closer to my family. But they just weren't ready to accept the life I was choosing to live for myself. Finally, when I bought the house, I was thinking of you with Asmar. We shouldn't ever have to worry about being prepared to take care of our kids." Pangi said.

"Were you really thinking of Asmar and me? You know you don't have to take care of us. We will be fine. Just give us some time to figure things out. We will make a life for ourselves, too." Tanya was saying.

"Oh, I don't doubt you will, but I thought it would make sense to raise our kids together. Sisters together. And you know, Geyali said our kids are related." They both smiled, remembering that. They were bound together.

Tanya couldn't know just then what the impact of her decisions was on her future. What was gradually dawning on her in that moment, what was welling up from some gushing spring deep in her core, was her special love for Pangi. Of course, this was where she should be! More than anything, during the time she was in the Mennonite village, she had missed this woman who had become her partner. Now that she was in her presence again, she felt as if a puzzle she had been working on for a long time had been completed with a satisfying click, like that last piece fitting into place. They heard the children laughing and scuffling upstairs. They looked up towards those sounds and then looked at each other. They got up and met at the end of the counter, face to face.

When Tanya looked into Pangi's eyes she could feel her pain about being rejected and estranged from her family in America. She felt her need. And when Pangi looked at

Tanya, she knew Tanya's deep-seated fears that love would never find her —and she knew what her partner needed.

"Pangi, I never thought about being with you, but I know that I never missed anyone the way that I missed you. I realized every morning how the sunrise was so different without you and how I loved the sun rising with you." Tanya said.

"That is understandable because for me the sun always sets with you. I missed our lives together."

There was a deep sigh and a settling in the house, as the children came bounding down the stairs and the two women took in the feeling of family and home and love. They stood with their arms slipped around each other's waist, and they marveled at the fullness they felt and how their communal cup was overflowing.

****

Tanya sat in the waiting room outside of the bishop's office, which seemed so much smaller than it had seemed in the past. His secretary came to the door. "Bishop Wilson will see you now, Pastor Stokes. Welcome back."

"Thank you, Susanna. It's good to be home." She answered.

"I can't wait to hear more about your trip. Did I hear that you adopted a little boy?"

"Yes." She reached into her bag and pulled out her wallet to show Susanna a picture of Asmar sitting on her lap.

"He is adorable!"

"Yes, thank you. I have more pictures, but I had better get in here and speak to my boss." She laughed.

The Bishop stood up to greet her with his hand outstretched as she entered the open door to his office. "Tanya. How are you? Please have a seat. He said as she shook his hand. "Can I get you something? A drink, coffee…anything?"

"No thank you. How are you?"

"I am great! It's busy as always but I am glad to have some time to catch up with you. You have had quite the global mission experience. And a lot of life changes. How are things going? Are you getting all settled?"

"Yes. I am. It has been a whirlwind! I have just been trying to get back in touch with my family and I had forgotten all about the demands of having a small child after all these years, but I am getting back into that, necessarily!"

"That's right, I am sure that is a challenge. I saw you showing Susanna a picture. Let me see the little lad." Tanya handed him the wallet and he looked at the photo smiling. "He is quite handsome. Is he adjusting well?"

"Oh, he is fine…getting spoiled rotten!"

"Well, that is to be expected. Like I said, you have had some experience and I am glad it has all worked out. Right now, I want to look at some ways that you might share the experience with the rest of us. We all must learn from your experience. Have you thought about that?"

"Yes. Margaret Fischer has me lined up to speak at some women's groups already. I am also slated to go to Chicago next month for a conference. I'll be leading a workshop there. I have slide shows, pictures, art, artifacts, souvenirs and what have you."

"Great. We are thinking we would like you to preach at the next annual assembly if you are willing."

MONA FITCH-ELLIOTT | 171

"Of course! I would love to do that."

"Also, would you be willing to lead a workshop on cross-cultural perspectives at our Multi-cultural Conference?"

"Yes. That would be great! I would love to have my partner Pangi Abassi do that with me. We worked closely in Cameroon, and we have put together some ideas for workshops around various topics that would be suitable for that kind of forum."

"Certainly." He looked at her intently. "This Pangi is Muslim I hear. I would love to hear more about her, and I look forward to meeting her. These perspectives can be of tremendous help in broadening the church's understanding in our pluralistic world."

"Yes, Pangi and I have taught each other a lot and worked hard to promote and develop more ideological tolerance of faith perspectives. We are eager to share that learning whenever we can."

"Good! Now tell me is this more than just a professional relationship?" He lowered his voice.

"Well suffice it to say that we have decided to combine our living situations. You know Pangi also adopted a child from Cameroon…a wonderful girl, Kiki."

"I see…of course, none of that is any of my business, but you seem happy and again I am very pleased that things have worked out so well for you. When you are ready let us know if you want to share more publicly about that relationship. That is up to you as you see fit. But as for these other engagements, I will have Susanna send you a letter of confirmation for the things we have discussed with the dates and we will go forward from here."

172 | JOBETH

Mia met her for lunch later that day. Tanya drove her Chevy mini van to downtown Philadelphia where her daughter had taken a job in the museum as a curator trainee. They were meeting at a coffee shop. Mia seemed so much older now. Her little girl was a woman of means now and Tanya was pleased with her progress.

"Hi, Mom. I am so glad you are back! Wow! I am proud of you, too. When I tell people about you, they are amazed."

"You are proud of me? Who is the mom here?" They both laughed.

"How is my little brother? I want to take him and Kiki for the weekend. We had a great time at the Franklin Institute last week, but I want to keep them for the whole weekend, next week, I have the weekend off."

"That is fine. Asmar is crazy about you? What's not to love? You give him anything he wants." Tanya scolded. "Of course, it's okay with me, but call Pangi, to make sure she doesn't have plans for Kiki."

"Okay." Mia quipped. "Besides you guys deserve a break. How is Pangi, these days?"

Tanya said. "She is fine. She is writing some non-fiction stuff about HIV treatment in Africa. She is doing great. We are doing some work together, too. Things are going well."

"Well, I also wanted to have you over for dinner, the two of you. Maybe you can come when it is time for the kids to go home next week. A dinner party in your honor... I can experiment on you with some new dishes. How about it?"

"Why not, we will be your specimens. Will you pay us?"

When they had finished their lunch, Tanya ran off to meet Elva at a meeting. It was the first meeting she had made since she was home. When she shared that she was with a woman, nobody seemed shocked. It seemed the important thing was that she was in a healthy relationship, and she was happily committed. It did not seem to be as important who it was with or what the gender configurations were.

"Remember what I told you, Tanya. Love is all around you. Are you happy? That is important. Love is not destructive… stay in touch with that."

Tanya had been around the world and back and she thought she had found what she was looking for and it all seemed worthwhile.

****

Gakauru's black hands were swollen, and his skin was dry and cracked in all the creases. His thick fingers grasped a torn and water-damaged photograph of him with his first wife Abina. He was much younger in the photo, and he looked strong and confident holding a staff and a shield that was hand-carved with images of ancestor warriors. His wife, Abina was beautiful in her ceremonial headdress, and her lips were stained with the color of red fruit. She looked happy, grinning with hope twinkling in her eyes. He did not need to see the photo taken by French missionaries to remember their wedding day, that time of peace, or their hope. The picture could not show the fullness of that time anyway.

He said out loud to Abina's spirit, "You are beautiful to me. My beautiful life!"

He sighed as he threw his head back and bit his bottom lip hard enough to distract himself from the pain in his heart. His youthful hope was buried in that pain, but was two wives ago.

Abina was a good wife, but goodness doesn't always last. When the area violence between factions escalated it damaged and destroyed their lives. Even villages that were not at war could not protect their women and children from their sons who were consumed by the violence. Boys and men were convinced they had a cause to fight for and that they could benefit from becoming soldiers. They were drawn to what looked like power, or adventure, and then they lost all connection to their tribal value systems; all allegiance to their families or any sense of community. They became mad enough to rape their mothers and their sisters.

After his pregnant wife was taken advantage of by some young militia, Gakauru held tight to the value system he knew. Gakauru found he could not stand Abina, after the violation. Even if the elders said it was not her fault and the missionaries tried to get him to remember his marriage vows and their unborn child, he just couldn't ignore the way other men were looking sideways at her. His dignity was wounded and tested daily. He felt bad when he sent her away because she was pregnant already with his child. He had sent her to the clinic in the village. He felt he had lost control and failed to protect his family. There was nothing hopeful or comfortable about their lives anymore. He thought he heard people laughing all the time and her eyes had a different look that he could not take.

He thought he would start over after time passed...time to forget. He did attempt to begin again with Fatima, who was a widow. He was glad she needed him, and the villagers thought he was noble to reach out to her. He started over with his second wife like nothing ever happened. When Fatima also got pregnant, he thought the ancestral spirits were blessing their union. Things were working out. Fatima was young and she would care for him. The village women told him his other wife, Abina had borne a girl. He thought that Fatima would make a boy child and she did.

As it was, Abina made a way in the village clinic community doing what she needed to survive, and she did not have anything to preserve anymore, just the need to eat and feed her child. She could take any humiliation after being raped and disposed of by her husband and after birthing a child who had no father. She was a woman without a man, and she was available for hire or the taking. It wasn't long before she was very sick with the virus. She was hopeful in the Cameroon settlement because she wanted to take her baby girl to a place where she would at least have a chance for survival when she was gone. A nurse in the village clinic was a lovely, smart woman who was darker than the Europeans and who also cared for Abina and was gentle with Kik, as well. Abina, knowing that she was suffering from HIV/AIDS, begged her nurse to see about Kiki and she promised she would. That is how Kiki came to be with Pangi.

Gakauru had imagined that his new life would be better than his life with Abina. When the village women emerged from the hut the night his son was born, a midwife carried the boy wrapped in blankets. They were not able to save Fatima. She had hemorrhaged profusely and her condition was already fragile. He had a healthy son, but he felt his hard circumstances were punishment for abandoning his first wife and the girl, Kiki.

So, he understood he would not be allowed happiness after all. He was so broken, he was unfit to care for his son. He would not dare try to build another relationship with any woman. Who would have him anyway with the curse that was obviously on him? He had heard of Abina's death at the settlement in Cameroon from the women who seemed to have a pipeline to everything that happened to everybody in the area. The grapevine of gossip was very strong. He felt responsible for Abina's troubles and he had nightmares about an emaciated and monstrous girl chasing him through the jungle. He felt old and broken after his tragic struggle, trying to raise his motherless son. Finally, he devised a plan: to take the young child to Cameroon where he knew his sister Kiki was.

He meant to bring him to his sister, but he was too ashamed. It turned out with him leaving the boy, in a bush, on the side of the road. He had assured the boy he would return. Then he hid and watched out, in the distance. He hid and waited, and it wasn't an hour before a black man and woman, the man with a British accent, and his lady friend, who was an American, found the boy. He was surprised that this unusual pair appeared. They had taken him away in their jeep. He was agitated and it was all he did to restrain himself from trying to get the boy back. But finally, he felt he was doing the right thing for the boy.

Gakauru was hopeless and filled with self-loathing after leaving his son to face an uncertain future. He stayed there crying for a time, as he was consumed in the agony of his tears and the hole in his heart. He knew his son would be better off, but he felt like a failure His guilt was about giving up or feeling like he was ignoring his responsibility. In the back of his mind, he heard the warnings that the warlords were getting nearer to the village. They were taking everything —burning and pillaging. They were raping, marauding and they had no use for old broken men. They stabbed and shot innocent people and left them to die in the fires when they were done. Everybody was starting to flee. There were warnings. But Gakauru did not run.

When Gakauru got back to his village he sat there in his hut, replaying his memories about his family in his mind. Where would he run to? Why? What would he save of a self that was destroyed so many times already? He was the foundation of all of his family's life cycles of suffering. He made up his mind how to end this evil attack on him and his family. Maybe his self-sacrifice would appease the hateful marauders and all the ancestors. When it got quiet in the village and everybody was gone, he was still there thinking of sacrificing himself. He heard gunshots and the loud shouts as the soldiers closed in on the village and then he smelled smoke and the awful stench of all things burning together. He was thinking of Abina's suffering, and his children's suffering, when he cried out. He cried out until the heat rose up around him and he was choked by the smoke. He dropped the discolored photo on the dirt floor and fell over on top of it.

* * * * * * * * *

THE END

ABOUT THE AUTHOR
MONA FITCH ELLIOTT

Mona Fitch-Elliott (68) was born in (Harlem) New York and lived in Jersey City, NJ from an early age. She attend public school and graduated high school (Ferris) and college (St. Peter's) in Jersey City. She worked in banks and corporations before she was ordained as a pastor (Evangelical Lutheran Church in America). She has attended the Lutheran Seminary at Philadelphia, Rutgers Newark, and Drew University (Madison, NJ). She was a pastor for 30+ years in New Jersey (Camden, Hoboken, and Jersey City) and has also taught school for several of those years. She has traveled to Africa on two occasions (South Africa, Namibia, Ethiopia). She is currently widowed and has one daughter. She currently lives in Hoboken, NJ, loves writing, and occasionally serves churches.

www.ingramcontent.com/pod-product-compliance
Lightning Source LLC
Jackson TN
JSHW071746130225
78994JS00007B/12